— THE BLOOD TEXTS —

YOU'D BETTER WATCH OUT

You'd Better Watch Out is a uclanpublishing book

First Published in Great Britain in 2024 by uclanpublishing
University of Central Lancashire
Preston, PR1 2HE, UK

978-1-916747-22-7

1 3 5 7 9 10 8 6 4 2

Set in 10/16pt Kingfisher by Amy Cooper.

A CIP catalogue record for this book is available from the British Library.
Printed and bound in Great Britain by Clays Ltd, Elcograf S.p.A.

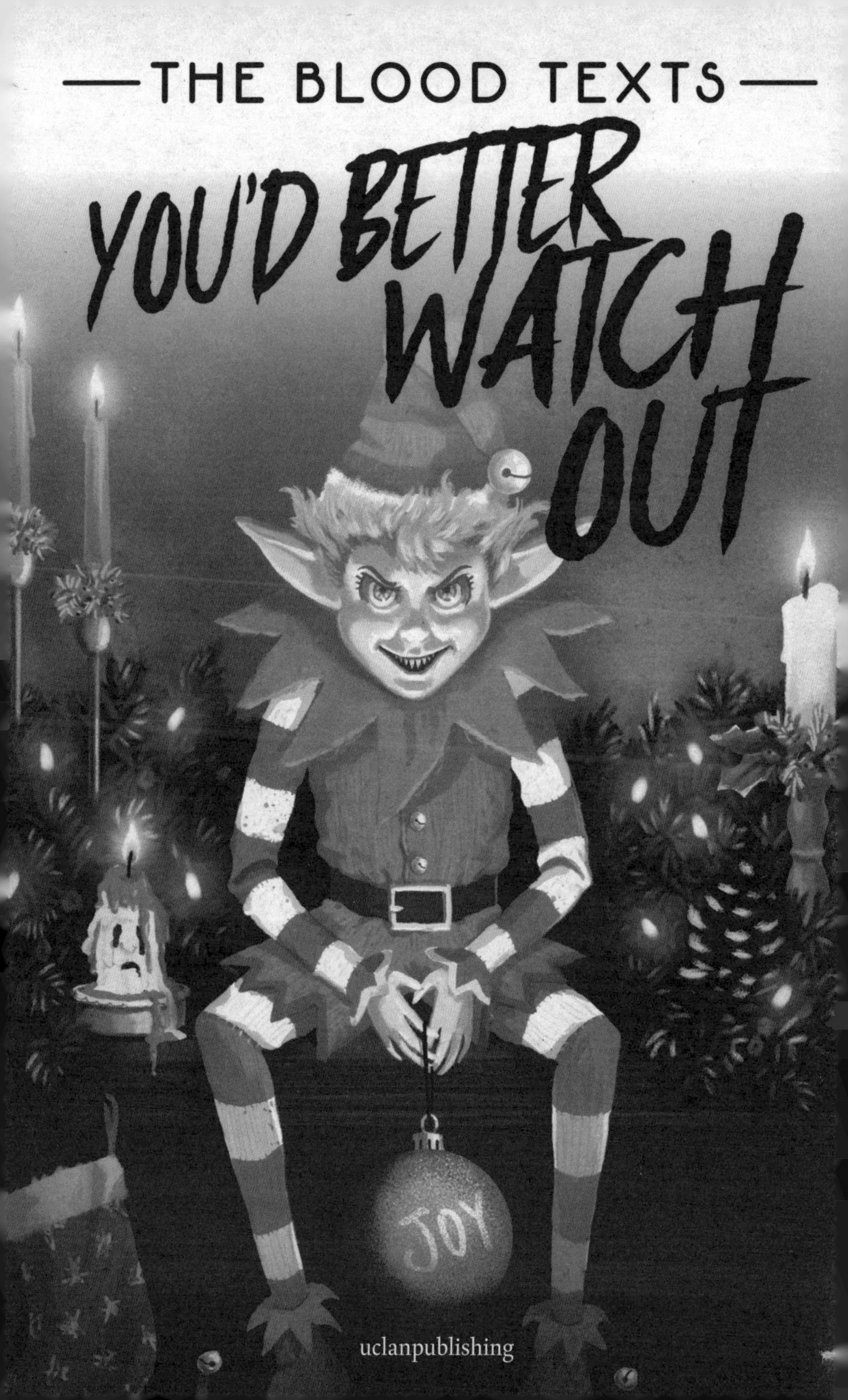
THE BLOOD TEXTS
YOU'D BETTER WATCH OUT
JOY
uclanpublishing

PROLOGUE

THE BLOOD TEXTS
2004 . . .

"You're scared."

"I'm not scared!"

"You're the one who wanted to do this!"

"I'm just saying, the coach is gonna go. We've got to get back!"

"Whatevs, run away then," Mason scoffed, his black Korn hoodie up over his ears, his legs straddling the metal track in what he would *never* admit was his *One Tree Hill* pose. From the path below, his friend sighed and turned away up the dripping, decayed exit ramp. As the New Animal rollercoaster rumbled far above them, joined by the muffled screams of its passengers, Mason couldn't help but call after him.

"Go on then, biatch!" he shouted. "Run back to teacher! But *I* won the challenge! *I'm* keeping the magazine! It's MY trophy!"

The magazine was tucked down the back of Mason's baggy jeans, and it was why they were here in the first place. *The Blood Texts* – the most gruesome and gory of his older sister's horror magazine collection. When he'd discovered a feature among *The Blood Texts'* creased pages about Smithson's Theme Park, just one week before their school was visiting it, he and his friend's next graffiti challenge had been clear: they would tag the *OLD ANIMAL ROLLERCOASTER, HOME OF REBECCA'S HEADLESS GHOST!*

"Rebecca didn't keep her arms and legs inside the ride. *Rebecca* wanted to wave to the camera. But once the 'coaster sped up, she started slipping out too far, and when the loop-the-loop went through the tunnel, her head clipped a boat on the old River Rapids. Her boyfriend had to sit the rest of the ride next to her headless corpse. After her family sued, Smithson's shut the Old Animal ride and built the New Animal over top of it. But *The Blood Texts* says they never tore the loop down. It's still down there, and Rebecca's ghost an' all . . . searching for a head to replace hers."

His friend had grinned then, and they'd gone toe-to-toe with sick jokes about the tragedy. It was what they did – like *Jackass*, like *Dirty Sanchez* – like grinning the blood out between your teeth after stacking a rail grind. Like sneaking past warning signs down an unmarked tunnel to graffiti the last bones of a deadly rollercoaster that Smithson's Park *didn't* mention in their ads.

MA$ON

He was getting better, he decided, as again the New Animal rumbled and screamed above. The dollar sign used to just look like he'd screwed up the 'S', but now it looked legit, like the $ in the rapper Ma$e. He leant closer to study it, when the battery light began to fade orange.

"Dumb torch," he growled. The batteries were the big Eveready ones he'd tea-leafed from his sister's new hi-fi; how were they failing already? Mason – *BANG* – smacked the torch with the – *BANG* – palm of his hand, trying to get some juice from the batteries, but the orange bulb still – *BANG* – wouldn't *BANG*—

Splash . . .

It came from below, quiet, but unmistakable.

"Tyler?"

There was no answer. Mason shone his torch down, lighting up twisted metal, bolts and rails, to the brown, stagnant water of the closed river rapids beneath. Seeing nothing, he turned to point the beam behind him. The grey fake river wound further down the gloomy tunnel, surrounded by knackered SM_LE _OR TH_ C_MERA! signs, tattered rope queues and decayed plastic animal models. Then, with a sudden thought, he looked up to where the last surviving tracks of the Old Animal twisted and climbed, before stopping dead against a concrete slab that Smithson's had built to hide this infamous deadly loop-the-loop.

Huh . . .? The screams. The rollercoaster screams, from the New Animal.

Why have they stopped?

Splash . . .

At the second splash, Mason whirled the torch back down again, a cold stab of fear in his gut.

There was nothing.

And then . . .

Soft ripples raced across the grey water, before a ride boat bobbed gently down the river below. Mason's mouth felt suddenly dry. The boat was filthy, worn and circular with seats around the edge and a wheel in the middle. The insides were strewn with something black and matted, and as he climbed down to the bottom rail, Mason saw what it was and fought back the urge to scream.

Hair. Long, human hair. And blood.

Mason pulled out the magazine tucked behind his waistband and stared at the picture on the open page.

"It's true," he croaked out loud. "*The Blood Texts*. It's *true*."

It was the last thought his head got to have.

The Blood Texts. It's true.

— Chapter One —

If anything, it's Olivia's fault.

Miss Faith's too. She's always had it in for me – while perfect Olivia always got the encouraging smile. Miss Faith *knew* I'd be screwed for her sad-act Christmas Special Test. Like putting Christmas in the name makes it all jolly. *It's a test, you silly cow!*

It's Miss Faith's fault, because if she hadn't of given me *that* look, then I wouldn't of felt that piece of coal in my gut. That anger.

I wouldn't of even *thought* to cheat.

And actually, it's Declan's fault too. Firstly, because he was talking so much about how his mum would get us into the cinema to see that new horror, *Slay Bells 3: Silent Night, Unholy Night*, that I didn't even know what this test was meant to be about.

Secondly, because when I nudged the fricking numbnuts during the test and nodded in Olivia's direction (who didn't have the decency to at least *try* and hide her answers), he got this big dopey grin on his face, and of course Miss Faith spotted it straight off. He didn't just top up his answers like I was doing either. That fool got himself a ten out of ten, *then copied Olivia's name onto his damn sheet before crossing it out!*

But what happened next was definitely Olivia's fault.

See, after Miss Faith saw Declan's test and rared on him (*"YOU ARE ONLY CHEATING YOURSELF!"*), she then made a big show of looking over *my* shoulder at *my* test, while the whole class stared, all judgey. Then, gutted because she didn't have any proof that I'd copied, she floated back to her desk with her posh-hippy hair and her kooky, crappy, *inspirational-English-teacher* clothes, and said, "The Ghost of Christmas Future was sitting by Evangeline Clark too, I see."

And there it was again. That anger. That little piece of coal in my stomach, burning hot.

Because I didn't really get her weak joke but I *knew* what Miss Faith was saying. She was calling me *thick*. And as the blood rushed to my cheeks, as my face burned hot from embarrassment and anger and . . . *hurt*, I saw perfect little Olivia turn forwards again, but not before catching a small smile on her perfect little teacher's-pet face.

Class ended, and I was still angry.

We all filed out of the classrooms, a slurry of teenagers in drab white and grey uniforms squeaking down halls decorated with the world's most depressing pound-shop tinsel, and all I had was Olivia's smirking face in my head, and that coal burning up my guts. It kept burning too, all through Kelsey's tragic attempts to flirt with Declan. All through Geography, every time Olivia shot a pale, nail-bitten hand up to answer yet another question. All through sneaking through the gap in the fence to the Derelicts for a breaktime vape when the coast was clear, and all through dossing about in French. By lunchtime, I was stood in the food queue, listening to tinny old Christmas songs coming through the tannoy and brimming with rage.

NNNNNope. I'm not having this.

"Turkey stew or Christmas Veg Surprise, duck?" the lunch supervisor asked, but I couldn't care less. My focus was on Olivia, saying her delicate *please*s and *thank you*s at the other end of the line. *She* should learn how it felt to be the loser. *She* should learn how it felt to be turned into a joke.

"You getting something, or what?" Declan muttered. "Ange?"

I ignored him. Olivia left the queue with a full tray, and I followed. With every step I strode closer, letting the rage boil my blood, my eyes boring holes into the back of her skull, until I was right behind and grabbing my phone out my pocket.

"Ange, what are you—" Declan called, but it was too late. As Olivia turned, I kicked out at her feet, sharply hooking my leg around hers.

She fell. *Hard.*

And she didn't let go of the tray like a normal person would. She clung on to it, not even putting her arms out to break her fall. Her food went flying – stew splattering up into her face – legs sprawling out so wide that the back of her trousers made a comedy *ripping* sound. All at once, the dining hall fell silent except for the dribbling tannoy music – *"I believe in Father Christmas! I believe in peace on Earth!"* – and everyone, on every table, stared down at Olivia Novak.

I pointed my phone at her. *Click.*

And right then, just as a perfectly focused shot of Olivia's horrified, gravy-covered face sharpened on my screen, just as I tucked my phone back in my pocket and *just* before Miss Faith barged angrily through the crowd screaming, *"EVANGELINE CLARK!"*, that piece of coal vanished like it had never been there.

The hole it left behind, though? Well, that's guilt. Because, let's face it, it wasn't Olivia's fault at all.

— Chapter Two —

"It'll be here . . . there . . . wherever you might cause trouble!"
my dad said angrily, and slammed the box down so hard the
kitchen table rattled and dust came off his blue work jumper.
There was a long pause where me, my mum and my kid sister,
Edie, all stared. And nobody answered, cos no one had the
right words for "*have you gone nuts?*".

The wooden box was old-looking with a glass window.
Scratched across the bottom in spindly writing it said:

The Watching Elf.

The Watching Elf was the thing behind the glass, a
wooden doll of a little elf about medium teddy-bear-sized,
except this was no cuddly little friend. He was *horrible*;
a flinty, violent-looking toy from the olden days. The kind
of creature that belonged in yellowing books of bloodthirsty
fairy tales, or the old washed out, box-shaped TV shows my
grandparents like; shows with evil ventriloquist dummies
and fauns in bad make-up that go around saying "rin-tin-tin".

His eyebrows were neat, *too* neat, little triangles that
were meant to look friendly and amused but . . . weren't.

His skin was snowdrop-pale and his cheeks were pinched red, and still somehow his face looked like it hid something much older, a skin-thin mask ready to crack and mould at any minute. His lips were thin and red, and peeled back in a smirk that was meant to be funny yet stern, a jokey *You naughty kids, you!* grin. But, just like his raised eyebrows, that smirk was quivering with violence and hate. This was made even worse by the teeth behind it. On a baby face like this, as unnerving as it was, you'd expect them to be pearly white and cheerful, but the teeth in the elf's mouth were yellowed and sharpened to jagged points, so real that if I'd leant forwards and opened the little door of his box, I wouldn't be surprised to smell stale blood on his breath. It was all so *wrong* somehow . . . and it was made even worse by the elf's chirpy Christmas outfit – from his dinky boots with bells on the end and his stripy stockings, all the way to the fluffy green elf hat that sat on top of his rumpled hair.

I peered closer through the glass, my mouth suddenly dry, and his cruel, smiling eyes gazed steadily back – a murder's worth of malice in their pin-prick pupils.

"It's the Watching Elf," Dad pronounced solemnly. "So you had *better* be good!"

I wanted to laugh. Dad's Christmas *mad*. Spends weeks decorating the flat in every tacky car-boot-tinselly tat he can find – but this was ridiculous, even for him. No way was I laughing tonight though. Thanks to his building site being *right* behind the school, Miss Faith had called him in after the whole ish with Olivia. By the time she'd finished sharing all her hateful propaganda about me, he'd come out her office with a mad, deranged look – a scary mix of desperation and rage in his eyes.

Desperately, I looked to Mum for support. She was fixing up Edie's costume for her Christmas Show and, to my relief, she didn't look too happy to have Satan's garden gnome in our flat either.

"We are *not* having that thing in here, Shay," she said.

"Let me look," Edie said, and I slid the box to her. As she stared at it, Mum turned on me.

"Do you see what your behaviour has done?" she said. "Your dad has *lost his mind*."

"I'm standing right here!" Dad said incredulously.

"Well, what am I supposed to think with you bringing that thing home? Aren't these elf things meant to be *soft*? Edie'll have nightmares!"

"No, I won't. I think he looks sad," said Edie simply. "Like an Itku Henki, missing his family."

We all stared at her. Edie's my kid sister, and even though she likes thrash metal, and dresses like the undead, and Mum and Dad have to make her turn all the crosses on her bunk the right way up when Nanna visits, she's actually a really sweet ten-year-old girl, always seeing good in people and the madcap imaginary world she inhabits half the day. It was actually her old Halloween outfit Mum was making Christmassy right then, sewing snowmen up the hem of her witch's cloak ready for her theatre club's big Christmas show. Tbh the snowmen looked pretty evil too.

"Anyway," Mum said. "I thought we weren't going to buy any more decorations this year?"

"I didn't buy it, I found it!" Dad exclaimed, eyeing Edie's snowmen with dismay. "We were clearing out a fireplace and it was just sitting there, like it was waiting for us."

"Urgh, it's from the *Derelicts*?" I said, and shoved it away. The Derelicts are these abandoned houses running alongside the school yard. They *used* to be the perfect place to skive, vape, make out, whatever you wanted . . . till my dad got a job helping to tear them down. He's been driving me mad – dropping me off at the school gates like a baby, and eating his sandwiches *right* near the gap in the fence.

"Tony said I should bring it back to watch over you," Dad said with a grin.

"You were talking about me at work?!" I nearly shouted it. "What about my privacy, Dad? That's so disrespectful, that is—"

"Don't start with that, Evangeline," Dad said shortly. "Not after today."

"I've been *punished* for today!" I shot back. "*Detention's* my punishment! Not this stupid toy. Like I'd even be *bothered* about an elf, like I still *believe* in—"

"HEY!" Mum and Dad snapped at once, both of them darting looks at Edie, and I groaned. Edie's their last baby, and me and my older brother Elijah open her eyes to reality on pain of death. Luckily, she was too busy murmuring nice words to the frickin' elf to notice. Finally, she looked up to see us all staring at her.

"What?" she said. But Dad turned back to me.

"She called it bullying, that teacher," he said in a low voice. "What you did. She said you *bullied* that Olivia."

Mum stopped sewing and looked up. Edie looked shocked; looked upset in a way I *hated*. I stared at my feet and wished for the ground to swallow me up.

"Bullying," Mum repeated. Her eyes met mine, and . . . and that was the worst part, because I'd never seen a look like it in her face before. Not disappointment – more like fear, more like devastation, more like . . . she had finally resigned herself to something she'd been dreading all her life. Finally, she put out her hand and said, "Phone."

I didn't dare argue. She took it off me and, like always, glanced up to her *super-secret* hiding place above the extractor fan. Then, when I thought that was it, she paused.

"And forget about seeing your friends tomorrow," she continued.

"Mum—"

"You're grounded for two weeks."

"But Declan's mum's taking us to the cinema!"

"AND I'm going to call this Olivia's parents tonight and invite *her* round instead."

"Mum, no!"

"And if, understandably, she doesn't want to come over, then you're going to go round there and apologise."

"What? That's stupid!" I protested. "Mum, she won't want to come and I'll look like an idiot and—"

"BULLYING!" Dad roared. And just as the Santa clock started to sing 'Santa Claus Is Coming To Town' for the billionth time that month, I shut up.

— Chapter Three —

"Hahahaha*haaaaaa*! You're telling me!" Mum shrieked down the phone.

"Mum . . ."

"Definitely no number then? Because I've . . . Ha*haaa*, like a shopping mall Santa!"

"*Mum* . . ." I gritted my teeth, batting away a frond of our plastic Christmas tree that *always* hangs over my end of the sofa. Mum looked up at the tinkle of baubles and I held the remote up hopefully. *Unmute?* I mouthed silently.

No. Mum frowned and shook her head. Sitting back, exasperated, I heard Elijah clomping up the stairs in his football boots. A moment later he poked his head round the door of the living room, tall in his kit, bandana matted to his forehead with sweat.

"Safe, safe, people—" he began, then saw Mum on the phone and stopped. He looked at her, looked at my miserable face, and whispered, "You in trouble again?"

GO. I mouthed right back.

He grinned this grin that *proper* gets my back up.

"In Trouble, innit," he whispered knowingly, and as I mouthed all kinda words back, pointing at him to go, he left. Course, Mum didn't notice any of this, she was too busy making that weird laugh she saves for other mums.

"Ha*haaaaa*! All right then – *haaaa!*"

"*Waaaaaah!*" I mimicked.

"I'd better go, she's giving me evils now. Yeah, huh, like I'm the one."

"What?" I said, mouth dropping open with outrage.

But Mum was smiling and deliberately looking elsewhere.

"See you tomorrow, thanks anyway," she said, and hung up.

"Can I at least put the sound back on now?" I said icily. "Or did you want to gossip about me some more."

"I want to gossip some more," Mum said without looking up from her phone, and I let out a silent scream of rage to the ceiling. But at last she stopped scrolling and sighed.

"I don't get it," she said. "None of the other parents have contact details for Olivia."

"She only started at the school this year," I said, and added hopefully, "Probably we should leave it then."

"Haven't you got anything? Weren't you two supposed to do a history project together – the family tree thing?"

I froze. How did she remember *that*? Olivia had been new to school at the beginning of Year Nine, and my history teacher Mr Taylor had decided for some terrible reason that *I* should partner with her on her first project – this loser 'Special Project' he'd got all teary eyed about – finding each other's family histories.

Ugh. And Olivia had driven me mental, trying too hard and asking me deep and meaningfuls about my family history, right back to Ireland and Windrush and everything. I'd meant to research *her* family, but the one time I asked she'd been all weird and vague, doing that whole pretending-not-to-care bit that I *hate* the Cringes doing, and so I gave up. Instead, at the last minute, before we were supposed to upload the history, I'd made a load of things up – saying she was descended from serial killers and all this other stuff which she *sorta* laughed at, but which Mr Taylor had a right bitch fit about (Detention #451).

Seeing I wasn't going to answer, Mum sighed again.

"Maybe if we search your phone."

"What?! NO! Mum, no, I . . . you said you wouldn't ever do that."

"I never said any such thing."

My mind flashed through screenshots I would *hate* for Mum to see – vape shots, snapchats and *hundreds* of messages throwing shade at Olivia.

> . . . lmao when olivias chair made that fart sound and she went brigh . . . . . . lighter fell out my bag and olivia looked 💀 shes cringe af . . . . . . cos miss perfect olivia says so shes such a bi . . .

"You – *no*, Mum. C'mon. I . . . There's private stuff on there."

Mum kept frowning, like my reaction made her want to check the phone even more.

Desperately, I thought of a way, any way, I could contact

Olivia without it. Then it occured to me.

"GroupMe!" I blurted out. "You can call from GroupMe! Olivia added me as a friend, I think. Here, give me your phone."

Mum's face turned stoney. OK, I said that a bit too abruptly.

"Please?"

With a sceptical look, Mum handed over her phone. I opened the GroupMe app on her home screen . . . and was greeted by a skeleton with an evil laugh.

"Jeez, what rabbit hole did *you* fall down?"

Mum let out a bark of a laugh. I *do* like making her laugh.

"It's Edie's account. She uses it as much as you used to. Are you even still on GroupMe?"

I signed Edie out and logged in.

"Hmm, not really," I shrugged, "but I still check it now and then." I tapped the Friends History option, this *long* list of statements like *Kelsey asked you to be her friend / You asked Kelsey to be your friend* appeared. "It's kinda pointless now, I guess. But you can call through it." I kept scrolling but couldn't see Olivia's name.

> Declan asked you to be his friend / You asked Declan
> to be his friend
> You asked Bex to be your friend / Bex asked you to
> be her friend
> Olivia asked to be your friend
> Raj asked you to be his friend / You asked Raj to be
> your friend

"There she is!" Mum said, but too late. I missed it and kept scrolling.

> Chris asked you to be his friend / You asked Chris to be your friend
>
> Olivia asked to be your friend
>
> Alanna asked you to be her friend / You asked Alanna to be your friend
>
> Ike asked to be your friend / You asked Ike to be your friend
>
> Olivia asked to be your friend

"She asked you to be her friend three times," Mum said quietly.

"I know, right?" I said, and *stupidly* still thought I could make her laugh. "I mean, read the room, woman!"

Mum didn't answer at first. Hearing myself speak at last, I looked up and saw that same look she'd had on her face when Dad mentioned bullying. It was that resignation, that sad despair. It was that dislike.

"When did you become such a . . ." she began, then looked quickly away.

"Such a what?" I said, but my smile was forced and there was a lump in my throat. Somehow, I knew what she'd been about to ask.

Mum cleared her throat.

"Let's call her then," she said, and reached over to tap on Olivia's name. "Where's the 'Call' button?"

"It's . . ." I began, then swallowed again. Olivia's profile barely registered. Where mine was packed with pictures and memories, Olivia had *nothing* from school on hers; not this school nor her last school. It was like she didn't really exist. Beneath her name was a figure that made me feel like a turd.

> Olivia is friends with 45 people / 6 people are friends with Olivia.

Only six people out of forty-five friended her back.

"Evangeline?" Mum said, and I hit Face2Face. Immediately the screen went to a black call screen – a dial tone sounded, and I handed her the phone.

"You speak."

"What? No, this is—"

"You want me to do this, *you* speak!" I hissed, and before Mum could retort the call was picked up . . . although the screen stayed blank.

"Hello?" Mum asked, surprised. There was a pause – still Olivia's camera never switched on, and then her voice came through, unsure.

"Hello?"

"Oh, uh, hi, Olivia! It's . . . I'm Evangeline's mum."

There was a pause. I rolled my eyes.

"Oh, uh, hi, Mrs Clark," Olivia said, sounding weirdly cheerful, "What, er – what—"

"I just want to say on behalf of Evangeline, *and* myself, that she – *we* – are very sorry for her behaviour today. Very sorry."

There was a long pause. Mum's eyes bored into me, willing me to say sorry as well, but I couldn't speak. This was just *too* cringe. Finally, Olivia answered.

"OK . . . thank you, Mrs Clarke."

"With that in mind," Mum said, still glaring at me, "Evangeline wanted to invite you round tomorrow to apologise in person."

There was *another* long pause.

"Is she waiting for you to say *'Over'*?" I snapped, but Mum pointed at me with an *angry* shush, and I shut up.

"I don't know if that'll work," Olivia said finally and I breathed a sigh of relief. "See, my mum—"

"Your mum!" replied Mum with relief. "Can I speak to her, maybe? I could collect you, and—"

"Actually, I will be able to make it," Olivia said quickly, and I swore to myself. "Tomorrow morning, yeah? Could you send me your address?"

"Great!" Mum said, and paused, a long pause. When it was clear Olivia wasn't going to say anything more, she added, "I'll see you tomorrow then! And again, I want to say how sorry I—"

"Thank you very much for the invitation, Mrs Clark," Olivia said politely. "I'll see you tomorrow morning."

"Great!" Mum said for the millionth time. "I'll send you that address now."

The screen cut back to Olivia's sad profile again, and there was silence.

"She seems very nice," Mum said finally.

"Why don't you just adopt her then?" I snapped back, and stormed out, mad at both her and Olivia all over again. Furiously walking towards my room, I stopped short. That stupid elf box had moved to the hall table opposite the living room door, shoved between a porcelain Christmas train and a dancing Santa. I picked the box up and paused.

Had he . . . *changed*?

It seemed crazy. But his horrible, yellowed teeth . . . were they really always bared in a snarl like that, lips peeled back to the blood-red gums? Those long, delicate fingers – had the nails always been so long and pointed? Had those peachy hands always been held up in front of his chest before, as though they longed to grab my throat and squeeze? And those glinting eyes, hadn't they stared straight ahead before? Now they were looking left, pointed directly into the living room as though this Watching Elf had been watching . . . me?

I slammed the box down face first.

"Very funny, Elijah!" I shouted, and stomped off to my room.

— Chapter Four —

I couldn't sleep that night. The guilt I felt about Olivia was chewing on my insides. Even worse, so was the anger. I heard my Dad shout "BULLYING!" and felt *so* ashamed, then Miss Faith's sneering joke echoed through my mind – *"Evangeline's been visited by the ghost of Christmas future"* – and I seethed with rage. The look of horror on Olivia's face as she lay on the floor of the canteen made me squirm uncomfortably, but then I saw that smile . . . that *smirk*, that BLOODY smirk . . . I had to do one thing; I knew I did. And to do this thing I *had* to get my phone back.

Without waking Edie, who was asleep in her bed across the room from mine, I got up, and tiptoed to the door, gently pulling it open. I peered out into the hall and hesitated.

The hallway was dim, lit only by a string of fading fairy lights. I've lived here for ever, can navigate this flat with my eyes closed, yet tonight it felt . . . different. The peeling laminate was icy cold under my bare feet as I winced my way across the creakiest floor in the world. The old woodchip paper on the walls looked faded and yellowing in the gloom, while the ceiling corner cobwebs cast big, wispy shadows that gently swayed across Nanna's cross-stitch nativity scenes hanging on the wall. Dad's old Coca-Cola Santa print came after, and where usually he looked all jolly and nice, tonight he looked warped – his smile creepy and cruel. Tonight, our home had become . . . unfriendly.

"Don't be stupid," I muttered under my breath, and tiptoed forwards. I crept past the untidy shoe rack, past Dad's tool bag, and when Elijah let out a loud *SNORT* from his room, I grinned, and my confidence began to—

Tap . . .

I stopped short, my breath caught in my throat. My body was frozen, but my eyes wouldn't stop searching frantically for the source of that sound.

Silence.

Nothing.

As my heart slowed, I moved forwards again – stealthily, slowly, past the open bathroom door.

Taptaptaptaptaptap . . .

It was the sound of claws scrabbling across the bathroom tiles, too light and quick to be human. Now I swivelled round, ready to run, scouring every shadow, inhaling the damp stench from the towels on the floor with every ragged breath.

"C'mon," I gasped, desperately trying to calm myself.

1 . . . 2 . . . 3 . . . 4 . . .

"C'mon," I muttered again, snapped on the light and prodded the pile of dirty laundry with my toe. Mice. It was probably mice. Dad says they come up from the flat below.

Was I really going to stare at towels all night, waiting for them to twitch?

See, I'm brave at things like this, I know I am. When it counts, I'll just put my fears to one side and act.

"Come *on*," I said for a third time, and carried on. Forgetting about stealth, I strode on down the hall, barged through the kitchen door like I hoped to catch something . . . and stopped. The room was dark, streetlights bouncing ghostly reflections off the oven's black glass, the only sound the *tickticktick* of the Santa clock. At least it didn't play that stupid song at night.

Carefully, I moved the dining chair to the cupboard unit and clambered up on to the peeling worktop, avoiding the plates stacked on the draining board. Gripping the cupboard door handle for balance, I got to my feet and stood on my tiptoes, stretching up to feel along the top of the extractor fan for my phone. *Ugh* – this was disgusting. The top of the cupboards is always coated with grease, and just then my fingers slid through a pool of it making me silent gag. But it was there, my beautiful phone. I lifted it down, wiped the grease off, and unlocked it.

Bathed in blue light, I swiped to my photos. It was the first one, and it made me breathe in sharply. Here she was, Olivia, sprawled across the floor, her mouth wide open *proper* gormless, her nostrils flared out and her eyes just *mortified*. It was the kind of photo that seems minor, then blows up online. A meme to ruin someone's life. I hit the three dots, searched down the options and found what I was looking for.

— 25 —

DELETE.

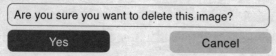

I stared at the tick and cross options onscreen. It was funny, this simple choice suddenly seemed massive, like a choice for my entire life.

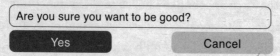

"Yes," I said, and suddenly a great weight seemed to lift from my shoulders. I tapped the tick and smiled. Then, suddenly, the screen on my phone fizzled to darkness.

And that's when I saw the figure reflected in the black glass. The figure standing on the floor behind me.

I froze, eyes glued to the darkened phone screen. The figure was standing by the table behind me, shaped like a human . . . but way, way, *way* too small. And its feet, no, they were . . . claws. Slowly, I began to turn and a high, unnatural tone came from the back of its throat.

I didn't even scream. Pure terror wrenched me backwards in desperate escape. I kicked out one foot, slipping from the worktop, bashing the draining board noisily on the way down, cracking my shoulder on the cooker and rolling off with a *BANG* on the floor. Scooching back frantically, I yanked myself back to my feet, ready to flail and kick and scratch out at . . .

Nothing.

There was nothing there. Silent whimpers bubbled at

my lips like a little kid as I wildly searched the room and edged towards the door . . .

Tap, tap . . .

Scratch.

Where was it?

Taptaptaptap.

This time, I did scream. The scuttling went right beside me and something brushed past my knee, making me jerk back into the table and then the wall – right into Dad's Santa clock!

"YOU BETTER WATCH OUT, YOU BETTER NOT CRY!

YOU BETTER NOT POUT, I'M TELLING YOU . . ."

With a sob, I burst out of the kitchen and raced into the toilet, locking the door behind me. For a moment all I heard was that stupid Santa song, then with the rapid beat of its deadly claws, the thing scurried back along the flat.

Taptaptappaapaparatatatapatatatapapadd . . . Until – silence.

Breathe.

Breathe.

It's gone.

But just as I closed my eyes, there was a

Stomp stomp stomp stomp . . .

It was coming back.

Stomp stomp stomp . . .

"NO!" I screamed.

"What? What the *hell* is going on?!" Dad yelled blearily from outside the door, and I fought back the urge to burst into desperate, hugging tears.

"Dad . . ."

"What? What is it?"

"I . . . I . . ." I began – and then weighed up my options. How would I explain being in the kitchen? And, even if I could, what would I even say I saw? Here, in the bright light of the toilet, it didn't seem real. I *must've* imagined it. It *must've* been a mouse, a creak, a trick of the light, a—

"Evangeline?" Dad said, his voice taut with tension. "What is it?"

"I-I needed the toilet," I said weakly, at last.

"I mean bloody hellfire, Evangeline. How bad did you need to go?"

— Chapter Five —

"The Watching Elf," Olivia said.

"Eh?" I replied, looking back from the living room door to see her *still* staring at that horrible toy. The elf was out of the box now, squashed between our weird 80s pop-out advent calendar and this other relic, a dictionary. "Oh. Yep. My dad thinks I'm still two."

"He got it yesterday?"

"Hm?" I grunted again. I peered out past the garland pinned to the door, but my mum was nowhere to be seen. Should I go now? Make a break for it?

"Your dad – he got it yesterday, did he?" Olivia said. "Where did he find it?"

"Behind some wall at his work. Made his damn day I reckon, until he had to go see Miss Faith . . ."

After I picked on you. There was an awkward silence, and I glanced back to Olivia. Her hair was all lank and knotted, her jumper moth-eaten and two sizes too small. I was supposed to apologise, I knew. But, after I'd ran out of the kitchen last night, I'd left my phone still lying *somewhere* on the worktop – and while Mum miraculously hadn't seen it yet, it was only a matter of time. I had to put it back in Mum's hiding place, and I was too knackered, too freaked *out*, from last night to listen to this Cringe dribble on about that stupid elf.

Not that I'd *really* seen anything, I'd decided. It was just a mouse.

Because mice stand on two legs, growling like some beast from hell.

"Has he tried moving it around yet?" Olivia asked. "Isn't that what you're supposed to do with elves? Move them? Like from there down to here, or something?"

"Why d'you care so much about a doll?" I snapped. "Of course he hasn't moved it around, he . . ."

I looked around and groaned. "Oh god, he has. It was in this wooden box in the hallway before. Look, he's even left the door of the box open. *Urgh*, that is so tragic it's depressing. He's even put it next to a dictionary, like the elf's learning English to ask for directions to the North Pole or something."

Olivia laughed, so loud and needy that it ruined the joke. I scowled again and she caught me, her face falling. I felt bad all over again, guilty, and annoyed too. It was *so* weird Olivia coming round here. Hadn't she guessed how painful this would be?

"Look, Olivia," I said finally with a sigh. "About yesterday . . ."

Just then, Mum's footsteps came up the hallway. She frowned at me, standing in the doorway.

"How's it going with our guest?" she said with a *you best of apologised* glare.

"Fine!" I said, getting lemon. "Why wouldn't it be?" With Mum I get mad, with Dad I cry. I don't even realise I'm doing it, but it works for the minor things. Too busy for a row, Mum waved me away.

"Don't give me the usual, Evangeline. I've got to get to work. Can I get you anything, Olivia?" she added in her nice, you're-not-my-kid-so-I-don't-mind-you voice.

"I'm fine, thanks," Olivia said, *nicely* back. I felt like a troll invited to their party by mistake.

"All right, then," Mum said. "Well, Elijah's at football and your dad's picking Edie up from Nanna's after work. Are you going to the park or something?"

"The *park*? Mum, nobody hangs around the park in *December*."

I looked at Olivia for support. She grinned . . . then ruined it by putting on this weird rude-girl voice that she couldn't pull off.

"I mean – yeah, it's completely *shiversome* out."

"Well," Mum said defensively, "if you *do* go out—"

"Mum, we're not going out."

"If you *DO* go out, don't forget your keys. I'm cleaning the kitchen, then I'm off too."

"Wait!' I said sharply. Mum paused, confused.

"What?"

Stay outta that goddamn kitchen till I've moved the phone!

"What is it?" Mum repeated, getting annoyed.

"I can clean the kitchen."

"You . . ." Mum said, and the corners of her mouth twitched. "What's happened?"

"Whaddya mean, wh— I always clean the kitchen!" I said, flaring up for real this time. Mum caught Olivia's eyes over my shoulder, shooting her a she's-only-playing-at-real-life smile.

"OK, Evangeline," Mum said at last with a grin. "Well, as nice as it is of you to offer, you should focus *on your guest.*"

That did it. She turned to leave and I dropped a bomb.

"You're wearing *that* to work?" I asked, as innocently as possible. Yup, I went there.

"What? Why?" Mum said, a defensive note to her voice. She's been on a health kick lately – all weird sea mosses and flouncing about to Zumba in the living room. Tbh the top looked fine, and she had the silvery extensions in her plaits that always look good. But I *will* shame your fat, hair, skin and filters, if necessary.

"No, it's just . . ."

"Your dad said it looked great, I'm almost back at my goal—"

"You're *really* close."

Mum scoffed, shaking her head like she knew *just* what I was doing. Still though, she pulled absentmindedly at the pinstriped sleeve of her shirt, as though to stretch it. When she turned away, she went left, *back* to her room to change.

I didn't waste a moment. With a quick, stern *stfu* look to Olivia, I raced silently down the hallway and into the kitchen.

For a frantic moment, I searched around the kettle and the slow cooker but I couldn't see anything. Then I glimpsed the screen poking out from underneath the microwave and breathed a sigh of relief. I slid out the phone, hefted up a chair, jumped on it like a flippin' ninja to put the phone back when . . . My phone vibrated.

Eighth notification this morning.

FOMO FOMO FOMO FOMO . . .

Still on the chair, I glanced back over my shoulder and unlocked. Declan had posted a video of him and my crew walking into the cinema – *urgh*, he didn't have his arm around Kelsey but she had her hand on his wrist and did this *stuuuupid* shrieky scream when he pretended to stick a screwdriver into his temple like Satan's Claws did in the *last* movie. Declan's asked me out before and I always said no because I didn't want to ruin our friendship, but still, we're close, and I've never liked the way Kelsey gets around him when I'm not there. Now they were going to be in a dark room together for the whole movie, while I was stuck here with boring-arsed Olivia and her boring-arsed questions. And then the *worst* thing happened.

"You really don't have to clean . . ." Mum began from the door behind me. I whirled around, my phone *stupidly* in hand. Her smile faded as she saw it, face clouding with anger, but not surprise . . . not any more.

"I didn't . . ." I said. But I didn't have anything to say. She held out her hand, and, too scared to argue, I gave her the phone.

"Looks like I need to find a new hiding place," she said. "Or . . . actually, I might just get rid of this phone."

"No, Mum . . ." I began, but she had already turned away.

"Take Olivia to the park," she said coldly. "We'll discuss this later." I was so *caught*, so red-handed, I didn't even come up with an argument till she was at the other end of the hall.

"All right, Mum!" I called after her. "Wish me luck with all the druggies and perverts hanging around a park *in December*! *MUM!*"

She didn't answer me, of course. She walked to the stairs out of the flat, pausing just to call back, "Nice to meet you, Olivia!" to the living room door. The front door closed; Olivia came out to the hallway. She was zipping up her rucksack, and she had a strange, guilty look on her face that looked *off*.

"Did you snitch? About the phone?" I began savagely. Then I remembered my decision last night and stopped.

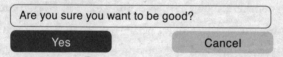

"What was that?" Olivia said, her eager-to-please face crumpling with worry.

"Nothing," I said finally. "Let's go to the park." *Urgh*, this being good thing was already crap and it wasn't even midday.

— Chapter Six —

The day wasn't all that *shiversome* (I mean, *who* says that), but it was grey, and the decorations on the houses opposite the park looked grim; pollution-stained Santas hung from windows, lights strung like barbed wire across bare tree branches. Missing my crew, dreading the penitentiary back home, I sat cool and moody on the swings. At least I *would've* done, 'cept I had Olivia, leant against the playground climbing wall, her gigantic school rucksack sat bulging beside her, talking *non-frickin'-stop*.

"... and so I was like, *no thanks*," she said, still trying her tragic billy-badass voice. "Like I want to do anything *more* about the Tudors? Do you have Miss Asgar for History? She sets these made-up debates, and they're just ... well, the last one was interesting but, like, not *really*. And she wanted us to do extra homework for History and I—"

"And you did it," I said flatly. Olivia faltered.

"What?" she said.

"You did the homework. Didn't you?"

Olivia nodded, her face reddening as she scraped the floor

with her plastic shoe. Jeez, it was Saturday and the girl was wearing school shoes. I complain when we go on holiday to the same caravan every year.

"Can't you ask your parents to buy you—" I began, but the gabby cow was already blurting out *another* question.

"You know that—"

"If it's a question about the elf, I don't wanna hear it," I snapped. But she shook her head.

"Well, no. Actually, it was about . . . that photograph you took."

This was it, the whole point of this morning. Suddenly, I found it difficult to look Olivia in the eye.

"Did you . . . yesterday, when . . . when you tripped me up in the canteen. Did you share the photograph?"

Staring at the ground, I shook my head.

"I . . . I deleted it."

"You deleted it?" Was that disbelief in her voice?

"Look," I said, still not looking up. "I've . . . I've made this decision. I'm going to be a better person."

Urgh, that sounded even more pathetic than it had in my head. This had gone too far, I wanted to take it back, or at least follow it up with the kinda stupid warning Declan would come out with – '*Don't take my kindness for weakness*' or something. But before I could say anything, a shadow dropped over me.

"What?" I said. Olivia was standing over me, a strange, unreadable expression on her face. For one horrible moment, I thought she'd try and bring it in for a hug, but she didn't.

Instead, she stood there like she was gearing herself up to do something. But whatever it was, the peace was broken when a voice called across the park.

"'Ange!"

"Isn't that your brother?" Olivia said. She was right, it was Elijah and one of his mates walking back from football practice. I couldn't help but grin with relief at the chance to get away from this *whole* awkwardness and, with Olivia left standing there looking *weirdly* annoyed, I hurried over to my brother. Unfortunately, his skeezy friend, Harry, was with him. Harry's in the same year as Elijah – not even two years older than me, but from his blue-ticked swagger, to the dodgy skinhead tattoos he initials on the backs of his fingers, to the weird way he leers at me . . . I *really* don't like Harry.

"All right, stink-breath," I said with a grin to Elijah. "Lose at football like normal?"

"*Tch*," Elijah said, offhand. "More like five-nil *the other way*, Angel. Scored a hat-trick. You playing with your dolls before you all dress up as princesses, yeah?"

I laughed, and flipped him a gesture. He's an idiot, my brother, but he's all right.

"I'll see you at home," Elijah said. "Going to grab a shower." But then Harry stepped up with a dirty look on his face.

"You can always hang around with me for a bit," he said.

"Woah, cuz," Elijah said, frowning. "That's my kid sister." I think it was the *kid* that got my back up the most.

"Er, *no*, anyways?" I said. "I think I'll chew on my own sick, thanks." Elijah began to laugh, but Harry looked angry.

"Don't talk to *me* like that," he warned. "Don't be disrespectful."

"Harry, man," Elijah's laugh had turned nervous. "She's facety, that's all."

"*Not to me*," Harry muttered, and as Elijah inched back I realised with a nasty surprise that *he* was scared of Harry. Not wanting any *more* trouble than I had in my life already, I tried to find a quick exit.

"Anyway, always a pleasure..." I began, but it was too late. Harry was staring past me, his face twisted in fury.

"Are you *serious*?!" he snarled. I turned, to see Olivia – meek little Olivia – standing there, looking terrified.

"Wait – what did *she* do?" I asked uncertainly, looking back to Harry. But he was *genuinely* angry. As if to match his anger, the strung-out Christmas lights in a nearby house began to flicker and fizzle out. Then Harry's face twisted in fury again and he swore, stepping closer.

"Wait, wait!" I said, *completely* baffled now, and stepped in front of Olivia. "She's not doing anything, what is wrong with you?!"

I've got this problem – I smile at the worst times. It gets me in so much trouble, because people think I'm laughing at them when they're angry... which, tbf, I usually am. But right then, Harry really was scary, stepping closer and clenching a fist. It was the *worst* time to imagine what some melt like *Olivia* could do to upset him. And even as my brain begged it *don't*, my mouth began to curl up.

Harry caught me grinning. His eyes narrowed. My throat

went dry. And my stomach dropped.

"You think it's funny?" He choked the words out, and suddenly I realised that this guy was a full-on *psycho*. With a snarl, he pulled back a fist and—*THWACK!*

"*OWW, shiii—!*"

I stared, completely gobsmacked. Harry hadn't hit me; hadn't done a thing. Instead, out of nowhere, something had got *him*. He was holding his hand tight to his face, covering his cheek, which was already blooming an angry red. I whirled around to Olivia, but her arms were stiff and down by her sides, her face pinched and pale. She hadn't thrown anything – I was sure of it.

But Harry obviously wasn't so sure . . .

"YOU . . ." he seethed. "YOU DUMB—"

But before he could finish that sentence, a *rock* flew out from the tree to my left at an inhuman speed, smashing into the back of Harry's hand.

"*ARGH!*" Harry shouted again, only now there was a sob to his voice. Frantically, I looked left and right. Who was throwing these rocks? Olivia stood perfectly still behind me, while Elijah looked ready to blub, stuck between helping Harry and running away. I was still looking when, all around us, there was a horrible, high-pitched growl.

RRRRIPPP.

I had heard that sound before.

"C'MERE!" Harry snarled, but he didn't even know where to look. "You, wait till . . . wait till I—"

He never finished that threat. *Another* rock flew out from

the opposite direction, smashed into his jaw and sent him sprawling. Again, the growl came, high and unpleasant, a knife scraping across a plate.

Now Harry was just whimpering, struggling to his feet. Blood began to trickle from between his swelling lips, and he let out a mewl like a frail puppy. I felt sick. I didn't like Harry, no, I *hated* Harry. But this was messed up.

"You all right, Harry?" Elijah asked cautiously, but Harry shoved him aside. *THWACK!* Another rock flew into Harry's shoulder and he let out a scream. Then another – *THWACK!* – and another – *THWACK!* – and faster and faster until Harry had collapsed back on the floor and was writhing in pain. *THWACK! THWACK! THWACK! THWACK!*

"STOP!" me and Olivia shouted at once.

And, just like that, the rocks stopped. The playground was ominously silent, nothing but the metallic creaking of the swing gently swaying in the wind. The three of us stood staring as Harry lay there, dreadfully still. Nobody spoke.

At last, Harry moved. He struggled to his feet, bruises swelling his face, spitting out blood. He looked wildly around, his fists clenched, his breath coming out in heaves and gasps.

Then, he turned and ran away.

We stayed standing there, the three of us – me, Elijah and Olivia, still not moving, still not talking. There was a sudden rustling in the bushes again, and we all yelped out loud. But there was nothing more.

"What was that?" said Elijah, breathing hard.

"Evangeline," Olivia said. "I-I think I need to get home."

"You sure?" I said. She was breathing hard and her eyes were animal-wide. For the strangest moment, I wondered if she would hit me.

"I'm sure," she said at last. Cheeks red, she zipped up her empty rucksack, half-ran out of the park and fled up the street.

"Is she OK?" said Elijah. "Shouldn't you—"

I cut him off with a shrug. My hands trembled, and I scrunched them in my pockets.

"She's not my friend, is she," I said. "Stupid idiot was more into Dad's stupid . . ."

I trailed off. Something *mental* had just occurred to me – something connected with drab Christmas decorations, with the unsettling patter of feet and that horrible high-pitched growl. I remembered the figure I'd seen reflected in my phone screen the night before. As impossible as it seemed, I suddenly recognised it.

"Evangeline?" Elijah said, my big-shot older brother, all quiet and meek for once. "You OK?"

"We need to hurry," I said.

That's when I began to run.

— Chapter Seven —

"Tell me you're joking," Elijah said.

"It wasn't in this box before," I whispered. "It *definitely* wasn't."

Giving me side-eye, Elijah reached past me to the living room shelves and lifted the doll out of his little ornate box. He stared at the Watching Elf, and the Watching Elf scowled back, showing no more sign of life than any other doll.

"Funny . . ." Elijah said, and frowned.

"What?" I asked, alarmed.

"Just . . ." Elijah continued. "I swear it just – NO! NO!"

Suddenly, the elf flew at his face, sending him staggering backwards with a scream. Heart lurching, I darted towards him, grabbing at the evil elf and . . . my idiot brother fell about laughing,

"Are you *actually* serious?" I growled. "I am going to KILL you."

"Oh, c'mon," he said. "It's funny! Think about it, Angel. What you're saying is that this elf doll attacks people. Why? Why would he even attack Harry?"

"Because he was being naughty!" I shot back before I could stop myself. Elijah burst out laughing again. He was really starting to wind me up.

"It's a good job he did, though," I added. "*You* weren't doing much to help me."

To my satisfaction, Elijah flinched.

"Whatevs," he said at last, all haughty. "Elves don't exist. You're being a baby."

I'll be honest, I was beginning to have doubts myself. True, the elf was gross – like, Annabelle gross – but he was still only a doll. And that scuttering noise I'd heard last night, that had been something with *claws*. Yet the Watching Elf had on these tinkly dinkly Christmas boots, green with bells at the top and fluffy insides made of dreams and snowdrops. They didn't look like they'd scuttle anywhere.

"Maybe . . ." I said desperately. "Maybe . . . maybe he *isn't* an elf! Edie called him something else – an . . . an Itchy Scratchy, a Hanky Panky, a . . ."

"Not 'Henchi'," Edie said with a laugh. "*Itku Henki*. They're old creatures, from a Time of Yore. They're in *The Blood Texts*. Let me just clear this *magicka* into my *Ominidium* and I'll show you."

Edie picked the grotty figurines off her desk and turned away, humming along with the weird gothy cover version of 'Carol of the Bells' that was dribbling out of her speaker. Behind her, I caught the grin on Elijah's face, and my heart

— 43 —

sank. I'd brought the Elf to Edie's half of our room in the hope that she'd back up my wild theory about it being alive, and already I was regretting it. Why had I ever thought my *ten*-year-old sister would convince Elijah I wasn't losing the plot?

See, Edie hasn't really got an . . . whatever an *Ominidium* is. Mum got these IKEA shelves on Shpock, and the legs were so warped she had to screw them into the wall to stop them falling over . . . only she screwed them too tight and as the shelves leant back, the front legs lifted off the floor completely. The minute Edie saw these shelves floating mysteriously a centimetre above the ground, she called them her *Ominidium*, the place she would store all of her *magicka*.

And *no*, I don't know why there's a 'k' in that name either. Or an 'a' for that matter. To be honest, nobody else in the world would ever look at this dutty old selection of Poundland toys and petrol station jewellery and call it magic, let alone *magicka*. I can't deny it though – the set of book boxes lined along the top shelf *do* look pretty cool. Six thick, red, leather-looking volumes, covered with magical runes and mythical languages. These *do* look good, I'll admit. *Magickal* even.

Until you open them.

"Hmm," Edie said, tracing her fingers across the ornate sleeves like some sorcerer's apprentice. When she paused, glancing back to us, both me and Elijah groaned at once.

"I got *The Blood Texts* off a strange owd woman on a dark, rainy day," she began mysteriously.

"It was a car boot sale," I cut in. "We were there with you—"

"She even *said* she was a strange owd woman herself," Edie continued determinedly. "She let me have all these mystical texts for 50p, because I had the *Aura*."

"Heh, that woman knew all about auras, Eeds," Elijah said with a grin. "I was standing downwind from her."

"What?" Edie snapped. She's sensitive about this stuff, and before a whole row broke out, I leapt in.

"Where did you see about this *Itku Henki* then?" I said, and took the first volume off the shelf. Straight away, she snatched it back and scowled at me.

"Not zero to twenty!" she said. "It's after the free ouija. Forty to sixty."

She hefted the first box back on to the shelf and continued to the third box along. With effort, she lifted it down and dropped it heavily on the desk Dad built for her, knocking a stack of *Take A Break* horoscopes to the floor (Nanna saves them every month for her which, don't ask me how that fits with church). She ran a finger carefully along the spine and, as fake as the old runes are, for one moment . . . For one moment the atmosphere changed. The music on Edie's speaker changed to another, creepier carol. The sky darkened outside, and the air grew cold. Suddenly, this whole thing seemed *proper*, seemed *real*, like Huggy Wuggy or Slenderman or Momo—

Then Edie lifted the book box lid, Elijah stifled a laugh and I felt stupid again.

"Now, which issue was it," Edie said seriously, a finger tapping her lip.

Because *The Blood Texts* aren't books, you see. They're magazines, just stupid corny magazines they don't make any more, actually called *The Blood Texts – MONTHLY MURDER AND MAYHEM!!!* The Strange Owd Woman at the car boot had sold Edie the entire sad-act collector's set, with five book-looking boxes to store them in, for 50p. Hopefully the woman used it to pay for some soap, cos Elijah wasn't lying about her aura.

"This one!" Edie said now, lifting the stack up to show a front cover with a cartoon of a *seriously* ill-looking girl. Running along the bottom – beneath the headlines *Five Uses for Hemlock!*, *"When I Was Cursed": Three People Share Their Stories!!!* and *TEKE TEKE: STILL ON PUBLIC TRANSPORT!* – was a list of creatures featured in that issue: Teke Teke-Banshee-Itku Henki.

Edie flicked through the magazine, past word searches, spot the differences and some *scary* looking creatures. The banshee was this grainy old phone snap of torn rags floating above a slasher-looking family on a farm, and Teke Teke, that ill-looking girl, had *half her body* chopped in two!

"Have Mum and Dad gone through these magazines?"

Edie paused and gave me a hard stare.

"Do you want my help or do you want to be a dobber?" she said, and with a sheepish nod, I zipped up my mouth. Satisfied, Edie turned the page and spun the magazine around to show us.

"Oh my gosh," I whispered. There, on the page, was the Watching Elf with a demonic, red-tinted madness to its eyes. In its hand was a dagger, deadly and dripping with blood. Oh, and it *wasn't* called a Watching Elf. Edie was right.

Itku Henki: The Murdering Moralist!
Similar Beasts: Yule Lads,
The Whipping Father

In the deepest, darkest woods of Finland, there once roamed henki. Curious, gnome-like creatures, possessed of a powerful magic and long sharp claws instead of feet, the henki nevertheless were known as peaceful beasts – drifting naked among the trees with no goal and no master, gifting the surrounding areas with their gentle songs. Yet, for one carpenter, a deeply pious man who lived on the edge of the woods, such a naked, carefree existence was an abomination of sin.

"I can change them," he said. "I can give them morality."

Ensnaring a henki with ancient local folklore, the carpenter was cruel to be kind. He subjected the poor fey creature to agonies beyond the reckoning of mortal men, flaying the wickedness from its physical flesh, restitching it into his own zealous image.

He succeeded in horrifying fashion.

Twisted and scarred by the ordeal, the henki awoke to find itself dressed in a pretty Christmas suit, stitched together with the same ghastly care as its soul had been.

"Good tidings, sinner!" the carpenter said grandly. "You awake . . . an elf!"

He gestured to a pile of wood on his one side, and a sack of mouldering potatoes on his other.

"The good children deserve pretty masks for their Christmas presents. You can carve them out of wood. As for the naughty children, they need a lesson as I have taught you. On this sack of potatoes is a knife for peeling. As reward for your new morality, I will let you decide which part of this gift the naughty children deserve; the skin or the flesh."

Christmas Eve came and, in the dead of night, the scuttling sound of claws through the snow to the village. He was monstrous, the carpenter, but not entirely evil, and as the morning approached, he grew excited to see the delight on those good children's faces. At last, the sun rose and, unable to contain himself any more, he hurried out through the icy cold to see the result of his work.

He had not gone far before a mother's shriek shattered the dawn.

For the elf had taught the bullies and brutes with the same cruel lesson he himself had learnt. The gift for the children who were good? They received their wooden masks, sure enough. But those masks were decorated by the stretched faces of their former tormentors, the flayed skin of the town's 'naughty' children. The carpenter had gestured to the sack of potatoes with a peeler on top, and had told the elf to decide which part of the gift they deserved. The elf had chosen the peeler, the skin and the flesh.

More parents came stumbling across the snow, their moans, their sobs, ghastly in the twinkling Christmas lanterns. And, too late, the carpenter saw that he had made a dreadful mistake in his gruesome education of the 'elf'. For alongside the flayed faces of those few genuinely cruel children, there too were the faces of the merely cheeky, those tellers of white lies, those doers of minor mischief – children whom the carpenter had himself always thought to be good.

The henki had never been taught this understanding. The smallest slight, the slightest sin. All deserved its terrible wrath. And as the carpenter himself staggered backwards in horror, the town lights began to putter out, one by one, and for the first time since he had captured the henki, he heard its ethereal song. Only now that song was not ethereal. Now that song was a foul and bestial screech.

Itku Henki - the Wailing Spirit

"I'm not finished!" Edie whined, but I couldn't wait. I turned the page . . . and frowned.

""What happened to this page?" I asked.

"What do you . . ." began Edie, then her face fell. "Oh, some of them are like that."

On the other side of the page we'd read was an advert for some old-fashioned clothes called Eclipse. But the next page along, where the article continued, had been half-torn out, leaving just a heading and the very bottom paragraph:

Surviving the Itku Henki

Remember . . .

1. The Itku Henki looks out for ANY wrongdoing: 'The smallest slight, the slightest sin'.

2. If the Itku Henki is following you, then it will be watching everyone around you:

your friends, your family . . . everyone. Take
care in the company you keep.
3. Being the elf's friend could be worse than
being his enemy.
And above all . . .
BE GOOD . . . OR HE'LL FLAY YOU ALIVE!!!
(Purchase three Itku Henki for just £16 from our
shop, catalogue number 466/3420)

"I wonder what that third one means," Edie said thoughtfully. "'*Being the elf's friend could be worse than being his enemy*'?"

"Oh my days, who cares?!" I said. "*What has Dad brought into this house?* This evil spirit will kill us all!"

"Dude . . ." groaned Elijah. "They've got a special offer on them. You can't actually believe this rubbish."

"Whatevs," I said, and snatched the elf from his hands. "You don't believe me. But *something* threw rocks at Harry in the park, and it wasn't Olivia and, let's face it, it definitely, *definitely*, wasn't *you*."

Elijah blinked. For a moment, shame crossed his face at the fresh memory of the park, of not defending us against his 'friend'. Then, like he was batting it away, he sneered.

"I can't believe you two are scared of something out of a stupid corny magazine."

"They're NOT JUST MAGAZINES!" Edie shouted,

catching him by surprise. "They're *THE BLOOD TEXTS*!"

"Oh, *ish*," Elijah groaned, holding his hands up and walking off. Edie didn't leave it though. She kept shouting, getting angrier and angrier, and as Elijah hurried out of the room, she followed. Soon I was alone, holding the Watching Elf in my hands, and staring at the last words in the article:

BE GOOD . . . OR HE'LL FLAY YOU ALIVE!!!

I was still staring when I heard the *tick*, like a clock about to stop. Edie's speaker, which had still been playing its creepy carols, made a twitching sound and died.

I frowned, looking down at the elf, and tried shaking his head. One eyelid half-closed, the head nodded slightly . . . and it remained lifeless, dead-cold. Except . . .

Except something was moving in his boots.

I heard it before I saw it – that slight scratch, the tinkle of his boot bells moving. But then, as I stood, a horrified statue, something moved beneath the brown leather. The laces began to strain, like the elf's feet were swelling and nothing would stop them. Finally, the scratching paused.

Then a claw shot through the sole of one boot.

"*ARGH!*" I screamed, and dropped the elf. A claw tore through the other boot as he fell, his hands bunching up into fists. Quick as a rat, he scampered to the door on all fours before stopping and standing to face me.

"Please!" I begged. And the words of *The Blood Texts* and Elijah came back to me. "Please, I'll be good, I *promis—*"

But before I could finish, the creature opened his mouth and let out a terrible, inhuman, *rasping* squeal. Then, with a scraping and scuttling of his long, sharp claws, the Itku Henki, the Watching Elf, was gone.

— Chapter Eight —

1. The Itku Henki looks out for ANY wrongdoing:
'The smallest slight, the slightest sin'.

_____

He's still there . . . Watching . . .

By Sunday morning I was a zombie. I was exhausted, and I was petrified. The Watching Elf was back on the living room shelf, inside his little box. I would have to be good – good like The Blood Texts said. Or I'd be flayed alive.

So I began to clean. I started with my room, but the idea of not being able to see the elf freaked me out too much so instead I cleaned the living room. I didn't get mardy when Dad made some sarky 'well, THIS is a surprise' gag. I didn't tell Edie to turn her goddamned grebby music down, even though it was blaring through the walls right where I was cleaning. I didn't stop, in fact, except to glance up at the scabby little monster standing behind his scratchy glass door, secretly hoping he'd leap out of there with a *Ho! Ho! Ho!* and say, "Well done, Evangeline. You've passed the test!"

But he didn't. Way too soon, I'd hung all the baubles

back on the Christmas tree and hoovered up all the fake plastic pine needles. I stepped back and stared; at the hanging Christmas cards arranged neatly on string, at Dad's beloved crib sat on the high-up shelves with baby Jesus back in the right place, even at the fake-flame tealights I'd changed the batteries in. I looked around this perfectly neat room . . . and my eyes stopped at the Watching Elf. Finally, my temper snapped and I strode up to him with a hiss.

"I'll stop you! Stupid elf idiot, I'll smash you up!" Trembling with rage, I yanked at the little door to his box. Yet even though Elijah had been able to easily open it, now it didn't budge. I tried to prise the whole box apart but the spindly old wood thrummed with strength, and when I lost my patience and punched at the glass with my middle knuckle it hurt like *hell*, brought tears to my eyes and sent me skipping round the room with silent cries of fury.

The glass wasn't damaged at all. Behind it, the elf smirked lifelessly at me.

"What are you doing?" It was Elijah, stood in the doorway. He was holding a fluorescent glass of squash and had that shadowy-eyes thing he gets when he's tired and hungry. (Nb, Elijah's an OK brother, but when he gets hungry? Then he's *awful*.)

"Nothing," I said, and put the elf back down. "I'm about to do my homework in here."

Elijah grunted. Then, like he hadn't heard me, he sat down on the sofa, *put his glass AND TRAINERS on the table I'd just cleaned*, picked up the remote and clicked on the TV. Instantly, my anger bubbled up and I geared up to say something harsh –

THAT SPOT CREAM STILL AIN'T WORKING, I SEE.

But then I caught sight of the elf watching me, that cruel smirk on his face.

Be good be good be good be good . . .

"Elijah," I said politely. "Can you leave the telly off please? I'm doing my homework."

Elijah looked at me like I'd smashed my homework over his head. Muttering under his breath, he flicked the TV off.

"Alexa!" he called. "Play Christmas songs!"

"ALEXA, STOP!" I shouted as some obnoxious bells jingled out the speaker. The music switched off and I prepared to tear into Elijah – *YOU MUST BE OFF YOUR F—*

Then I saw the elf. His head had turned, I was sure of it! Just a little . . . just enough to get a better view of what I was going to do next.

I stood there, my mouth turned down, fighting back tears.

Be good be good be good be good . . . One, two, three, four . . .

"Elijah, I'm doing my homework," I said through a strangled throat. "You have your tablet in your room. Can you *please* listen to your music on your headphones instead. *Please.*"

Something strange happened next. Normally all this would've been a cue for me and Elijah to have a screaming row. But new, calm Evangeline? He couldn't cope with that. He looked at me with absolute fury, more than he'd ever had when I lost my temper with him.

"What funny mood are *you* in?" he muttered. Then, with a huff that I think sounded *much* louder than he wanted it to, he flounced out of the room. I stood in the middle of my pristine living room, surrounded by twinkly lights, cards on string, a happy tree and the nativity of a silent night.

That's when the Christmas tree lights went out.

Then I heard it.

And my veins ran cold.

Drip ... Drip ...

Filled with dread, I went back to the shelves. There was no doubt now, the Elf's head was turned towards me. His blood-red lips were peeled back in a snarl, those yellowing, jagged teeth clenched tight enough to grind. The tips of his boots were stretched, those claws straining to get out. And his fists were squeezed so tight, so violent, that drops of deep red blood were falling from them with a *dripdripdrip* on the stained wooden base of the box.

"I can't even watch a stupid film—" Elijah began from the doorway, and with a deafening *CRASH* the high shelves above him collapsed – all the photos and books and ornaments piling down on Elijah's skull.

"Elijah!" I shouted, and ran over to him. Blood was seeping from a thin cut across his hairline and his face was a horrible pale grey. "Elijah ... MUM! DAD! MUM!"

I crouched there, tears filling my eyes, as my parents ran down the hallway shouting. Elijah stirred, his face unnaturally pale. I gripped his hand, pleading for him to be OK ... and then picked that moment to look up.

There, in his box across the room, the elf stared straight ahead, his fists unclenched, his teeth no longer bared. He was smiling.

— Chapter Nine —

2. If the Itku Henki is following you, then it will be watching everyone around you: your friends, your family . . . everyone. Take care in the company you keep.

———

"Ey, Ange!"

Keep walking.

"Angel!"

"Evangeline! Ange!"

Keep walking . . .

"Safe Angel! Angel! ANGE—"

"What is it!" I snapped, turning around at last. My gang stopped short – Patrick and Emma to the sides, Declan and Kelsey in the middle. Declan stepped back, scowling and looking (bless him) hurt. But Kelsey didn't blink an eye. Already she'd double-folded the collar on her uniform shirt, had put on more make-up than we're supposed to. It was like an extra warning – a reminder why I couldn't hang around with this lot today, not if the Itku Henki was following me.

"Don't give me that bish," she said coldly. "We tried calling you yesterday."

"I didn't have my phone!" I protested. "My mum's being a proper . . ." *Be good be good be good.* "She took my phone away. I had to have Olivia around and apologise to her for everything!"

"Urgh, Sweatycrack?" Emma said and I grimaced again – *I'd* come up with that name after this time in PE when . . . It's not something I'm proud of, anyway. "How was she then, boring as f—"

"DON'T," I interrupted. "Just – don't call her that. She was fine. It was fine. But then my brother's mate got . . . bad in the park, and then Elijah was hurt—"

"Hurt!" said Declan, his eyes widening. "What, in the park?"

"No, not . . . Some shelves fell on him and it was just . . . Look. It was just a *really* bad weekend."

Finally, my friends started to look more sympathetic. Well, all of them except Kelsey. Our relationship is kind of complicated. She's supposed to be my friend, *but* . . . she's also kinda my worst enemy. In a way, she's the one person in the whole crappy school I *don't* wanna piss off.

"Your brother seems OK now," she said sceptically, nodding to the entrance.

Sure enough, Elijah was there. Mum had dashed him off to hospital and they'd shaved his hair, but he hadn't even needed stitches. Now he was lapping up sympathy from his latest girlfriend, Stephanie, as she stroked his head.

"Yeah, it looked worse that it was," I said. "But I still—"

"We were calling you all the way up the alley," Patrick said.

"Eh?" I said. *Eesh*, it was only the morning but his eyes were already glassy. Patrick's smart as, but his mum's always away with her biker mates and he does what he wants. Tbf it's probably why we've never classed him as a Cringe even though he gets As and even works the decks at school shows and Edie's beloved theatre club.

"You said you couldn't answer the phone," he said in that cloudy way he has. "But we were calling you all the way up the alley."

"*All* the way up," Declan joked. Me and Kelsey rolled our eyes and grinned at each other. It was going to be hard, this was. But I couldn't let what happened to Elijah happen to my friends.

"I didn't hear you."

"Shut up, you didn't," Kelse said. OK, so she was making it easier.

"Look, I just . . . I got in real trouble on Friday," I said. "I can't really be . . . I just can't get in trouble today."

"Yeah," Declan said, nodding seriously. "Yeah, I get that. No trouble."

He means it, that's the worst thing. Declan is good, like, he has a *decent* heart. But he has no willpower at all. In an hour, I knew he would be trying to get me into some nonsense and then what would happen?

Kelsey though, Kelsey is smart.

"That's not what she's saying," she said, her voice

dangerously soft. "She's not hanging with us, because she thinks *we'll* get her in trouble. Evangeline is too good for us now."

"I . . ." I felt guilty now.

"It's about what happened on Saturday, innit?" Kelsey demanded. I stared at her, baffled. Declan had stepped back, uncomfortable, but behind Kelsey's anger there was a hint of satisfaction.

"Kelse . . ." Declan said, looking awkward.

"No," Kelsey insisted. "It's not like we planned it. The movie was weak *as*, and we've been getting closer for a while. You can't *help* who you fall for."

"Can't help who . . ." I repeated, baffled. Then, suddenly, I got it. "You two, on Saturday . . ."

"We just made out," Declan muttered. Kelsey's nostrils flared and she turned to him. He shrugged, even more awkwardly. After everything that had happened – the attack on Harry, and Elijah, this suddenly seemed so, so . . .

So *childish*.

I felt a smile twitching and had a sudden image of the smile Mum had given Olivia when I suggested that I could clean the kitchen.

"Honestly," I said. "I didn't know about this before. But *honestly*? I actually don't care. I still can't hang out with you – your *kiss* has nothing to do with it."

I turned away again and walked through the school gates. There was a gap in the crowds of students, a clear path with nobody on it. That was the route I would be following all day.

"We'll sit together in Spanish, yeah, Ange?" Declan called after me. I didn't answer, but then I heard Kelsey's hissed whispers, either explaining what I meant or criticising him for caring, and I paused.

A small part of me, the part that *did* care and *had* liked Declan and still wished, *wished* I hadn't tripped Olivia up and *had* gone to the movie with them on Saturday – that part made me turn back and yell to Kelsey.

"Congratulations, Kelsey. You've wanted this for *ages*."

There it was, that smirk of satisfaction again on Kelsey's face. Right before she turned to see a look of slow dismay forming on Declan's face. When she looked back, I knew that I'd turned my friend into an enemy. I just had to hope it wasn't for long.

So, I was good.

I sat near the front with the Cringes in Spanish, ignoring the baffled hurt on Declan's face when he wound up sitting on his own. I remembered that I had detention with Miss Faith later and borrowed *A Christmas Carol* from the library (she always makes us read our class book in detention), ignoring the two older kids winding up the librarian even though it was funny af. I listened in class and didn't tell my neighbour to get the hell away from me when he burbled, '*Shall, er . . . we work, er . . . together on, er . . . this?*' during Science.

And you know what? It wasn't that bad a day!

I mean, let's not get all misty-eyed about learning here –

I really missed my friends. My neighbour – I think his name was 'Thingy' – bored the life out of me, and when Declan got sent out for drawing penises in a biology book at the back, I felt bad for not being there to stop that poor dum-dum from getting caught messing up *again*. And as Kelsey and Emma's cackling laughter about a boy they thought had skidmarks wafted through the library doors, I *longed* to be cackling with them.

But not being in trouble was *so nice*. For the last lesson of the day, Maths, I went all out and sat at the front, right next to Olivia. My Maths teacher, Miss Acres, is all right, in a grizzly, *I-was-teaching-when-they-used-to-cane* kinda way, and when I answered two questions about sin cos and tan correctly on the trot, she arched one eyebrow and said, "Slaughtered *again* by Ms Clark!". Which from her, seemed like a medal. I was so pleased that at the end of class I lingered by the desk, desperate to share my big news with somebody.

"I'm going to be less difficult," I said proudly, before I heard somebody walking out and winced – *who heard that*? I glanced over my shoulder, and relaxed – it was just Olivia. When I turned back, Miss Acres was smiling, nearly poking my eye out with her madcap teeth.

"George Bernard Shaw said that 'the reasonable man adapts himself to the world; the unreasonable one persists in trying to adapt the world to himself. Therefore, all progress depends on the unreasonable man'," she said. "But he couldn't even be bothered to mention women, so maybe he can sod off, eh?"

OK, I had no frickin' idea what she was on about. Still, as I walked out of school I felt good about myself in a way I hadn't for a while. Outside was dark and grey, the shadows long across the front steps. A piece of the school's ropey Christmas tinsel clung desperately to the handrail, blown about in the wind with spits of cold rain. I looked right, to the Derelicts shambling behind building site barriers. Somehow, a mad psychotic elf had been hiding out there, till my dad had found it. Now, in this Grimmest Christmas Ever, it watched me, eager to slit my throat if I misbehaved. Was there a chance I could swerve it? Less arguments. Fewer detentions. Miss Acres's bonkers praise. Could this be a good life . . . being good?

It's a lonely life, a voice said in my head. My spirits began to slip again . . . then I heard the *clop clop* of plastic shoes, and Olivia hurried down the steps past me.

"Olivia!" I called. "Hey, Olivia!"

OK, I'll admit, I wasn't exactly speaking to her for her sake. Olivia was the only person I could think of who was genuinely good enough that I didn't have to worry about the elf attacking us. *She'll be my good friend,* I decided. *Two good, boring friends together, who don't get shredded to pieces by the Itku Henki.*

Trouble was, Olivia wasn't on the same page. Her mouth didn't shift from that drawn down thing it does, and as I hurried up to her, waving like some sad-sack stan, I swear she straight up avoided my eyes.

"Who died?" I laughed and thought, *Jaysus, don't tell me*

someone actually died. "Ignore me – how's it going? You ran off on Saturday, how weird was all that with Harry?"

Still Olivia didn't meet my eyes.

"Oh, hi, Evangeline," she said listlessly, ignoring my question. "What are you up to?"

A glint of anger stabbed at my good mood. She was *still* lucky I was talking to her.

"Nothing much," I said, my tone colder. "You?" *Why won't you meet my eyes?!*

"Nothing much," she said. "I mean, there's a rehearsal for the Christmas Show tomorrow, but I'm only backstage, like just putting drinks out and stuff, so I don't really need to—"

"Aw, it's the BFFs!" a sneering voice said. I turned and saw Kelsey walking down the steps with Declan, his hand in hers.

"Don't look at her, Dec," she crowed. "Evangeline's above us now. She only hangs out with the . . . what was it she used to call them? Oh yeah, the *Cringes*."

I didn't reply. Olivia, looking more uncomfortable than ever, made to walk away. Declan ignored Kelsey, which made me *really* miss his stupid arse, and smiled ruefully.

"I got kept behind for drawing di—"

"I heard, Declan," I said, and grinned with sympathy. He grinned back, the plonker. Kelsey didn't like that.

"Come on, Dec," she said. "Evangeline doesn't like us now. She wants to spend time with *Sweatycrack*."

"Kelsey, just shut up," I said quietly.

"I'm just saying," Kelsey said, getting meaner. "Like, it's a bit weird, innit Olivia, that she rejects us and goes with you the Monday after she was in trouble for—"

"Oh no," I said, and at least that shut her up. But I couldn't believe I'd been so *stupid*. "No, *no*!"

"Wassup?" Declan said.

"No!" I shouted in horror and raced back up the steps. "My detention!"

— Chapter Ten —

It sounds cooler than it is, the Media Lab. Maybe it would be cool if my teachers used it properly. At the front of the class is this big lightboard, a heavy desk in front of it that pulls out to show a control panel. We could FaceTime with real French kids on this thing, go diving in VR, probably. But no. Mr Simpson just plays us the same crackly French phrases – *Jules went to the park. It was good* – while Mr Judd doesn't even get that far and just mutters curses and jabs at the buttons while the screen shows everything but his beloved freeze thaw action. I swear his Facebook page came up once. And so, without a proper use for it, our futuristic Media Lab has become the detention room.

I raced in there now, saw one other kid in the room – this grotbag everyone calls Gold-digger because he picks his nose so much – and breathed a sigh of relief.

I'm not late! I'm not—

"You're late, Evangeline," Miss Faith's hostile voice said from the corner of the room, and my heart sank.

"Sorry, Miss," I said. "I was talking to Miss Acres and—"

"You were in trouble with her, you mean."

Look, it wasn't her fault I was mean to Olivia the Friday before. I'm not blaming her for messing up that day – or all the many, *many*, other days I get into trouble. But Miss Faith *does not* like me. She's actually a really popular teacher, always talking about these big, *good*, things like our 'emotional wellbeing' or 'personal growth' . . . but when I try to do well, she has this tiny little sneer like I'll stop trying soon. When I answer a question, she smiles to herself like she knew my answer was wrong before I even said it. And the second I look out the window, or joke with Declan, or screw up somehow, she gets instantly angry with me, like she was waiting to tell me off. She *hates* me.

"Right," she said now. "Your detention is starting from now – although obviously Evangeline can stay a few extra minutes. Because I want for this to be a growing experience, please take out your reading books and read for the next hour. Is this OK?"

"Yes, Miss," we said. She's always doing that – asking if everything's OK, like we have a choice. Once I'd said 'no' to one of her tests and she'd replied that it was fine . . . but then gave me a job sorting out everyone's marks which took up half my break instead. Now I opened my bag, reached in to get the copy of *A Christmas Carol* I'd borrowed from the library . . .

And paused. The book wasn't in there.

Setting my face, I looked again, more frantic this time. Inside I was groaning – *why'd this have to happen now?* – but after not finding the book for a second time, I kept my cool and took out my maths homework instead. I was just about to start work when a shadow loomed over me. It was Miss Faith. In her hand was a dusty old red book.

"I don't think that's a reading book, do you?"

"Er – no Miss. I had my reading book but I can't find it now."

Miss Faith raised an eyebrow. Nearby, Gold-digger was lazily graffitiing his desk, one finger practically grazing his brain. But she didn't even glance at him.

"Not a problem," she said. "But I do view these detentions as an opportunity for us to grow, Evangeline. Why don't you try to read this instead?" With that, she placed the dusty old book on my desk. It had a leather cover and yellowed pages. I had to peer closely just to read the writing . . . and then I realised that was the title! *Crime and Punishment*, it said, and the writing on the next page was even smaller still.

"Er . . ." I began to say. *I can't read this.*

"Everything OK?" Miss Faith said expectantly. She wiped the corner of her mouth and stared me out, a slight, sly smile on her face. No. There was no way was I going to complain.

"Thank you, Miss," I said, and stared at the book as she returned to her desk.

It was torture. The tiny words merged together across the page, spelling out a weird, olde-worlde English that made no sense.

My eyelids drifted together . . . My vision blurred . . . "*Excellent* job, Evangeline," Miss Faith said loudly, and I jerked awake.

"Miss, I—"

"Everybody else is able to use this time to explore and expand. You couldn't manage ten minutes."

"I didn't . . . I—"

"I'm afraid we'll have to have you here again tomorrow."

"Please, that's not—"

"Same time, same book."

"This stupid book!" I shouted it. "It's like reading the back of a shower gel! You haven't said *owt* to Pick-a-nose, I mean, what's he even . . ." I marched over and grabbed Gold-digger's magazine. "He's reading a *comic*!"

"It's a graphic novel," Gold-digger shot back.

"It's flipping Marvel Avengers!"

"EVANGELINE CLARK!"

Miss Faith proper shouted that, and at last I stopped. Breathing hard, she stood up and took several steps towards me. There was a funny look on her face now, something almost . . . hungry. Again, she dabbed at the corner of her mouth.

Suddenly, she turned to Gold-digger.

"You can go home."

"Home?" Gold-digger repeated in disbelief, his bogey-picking finger quivering like an antenna.

"That's what I said," Miss Faith snapped. "Unless you'd like to stay longer?"

"No, Miss!"

As Gold-digger hurried out, Miss Faith turned back to me. Again, she dabbed at the corner of her mouth.

"You know," she said, as Gold-digger's footsteps faded

away. "In the conferences I attend, we talk about the need to protect children – about their anxieties, about their voice. I'm a big supporter of that. That's why I've won commendations. That's why everyone believes what I say. But sometimes, very, *very*, rarely, I meet a child who is just too . . . problematic."

I breathed out and didn't quite breathe in again. The classroom lights flitted, like they were on the blink, but I barely noticed. Somehow the way Miss Faith said 'problematic', it was harsher than anything me or my brother or Kelsey has ever said, even in our worst row. It was like I was beyond fixing.

"Sometimes," Miss Faith continued, "I have to take matters into my own hands. Not because I want to. Because you just won't amount to anything, Evangeline Clark. Because the best thing for problematic people like you is—"

"MISS FAITH."

A boy's voice crackled through the speaker, making us both jump.

"What?" Miss Faith muttered. Staring hard at me, she walked to the front desk and pulled out the heavy control panel drawer. She was still staring at it when . . .

"MISS FAITH DIDN'T LIKE ME, SHE—"

With a rapid *slap*, Miss Faith hit pause and the voice stopped.

"Who's that, Miss?" I dared to ask. Miss Faith didn't answer. But she now looked disturbed.

"MISS FAITH DIDN'T LIKE ME, SHE—" The boy's

voice came through again, and this time Miss Faith *pounded* the pause button.

"Right," she said shakily. "I think maybe we'll—"

"MISS FAITH DIDN'T LIKE ME, SHE—"

Miss Faith SLAMMED pause again.

"SHE GOT ME KICKED OUT AND—"

SLAM, she hit pause again but the voice kept going.

"I TRIED TO DO BETTER BUT SHE DIDN'T WANNA KNOW, SHE SAID I WAS PR—"

With a choked, desperate noise, Miss Faith leant down and starting pulling at the plugs, snatching every wire out she could. There was a quiet mewl. The speaker switched off. The voice stopped . . .

And all the lights went out.

—Chapter Eleven—

"What?" Miss Faith said, silhouetted and scared. "Why are the lights off?"

I didn't answer. My eyes adjusted, shapes appearing in the dark; Miss Faith stood by the control panel, desks and chairs, *something scuttering across the floor.*

"What did you do?" Miss Faith said. I blinked, surprised.

"Wait, what?" I sputtered.

"WHAT DID YOU *DO*, EVANGELINE CLARK?!" Miss Faith strode around the desk and headed straight for me, causing me to flinch back. But then the screen gave a loud, horrible *POP!* . . . and we both froze.

"What is it?" Miss Faith, fear in her voice. "What's happening?"

I didn't answer, but stared past her at something *impossible* at the front of the classroom. Miss Faith turned too, and a dread silence fell over the both of us.

There, sitting in the front row, head in his hands, was a boy who hadn't been there before.

"Who's that?" Miss Faith said, and the childish whine

to her voice made me even more afraid.

There was another, horrible *POP!*, and the screen flickered violently.

Now the boy was sitting up. And with a grating crackle, his voice blared through the speaker.

"PROBLEMATIC, SHE SAID. COULDN'T GET IT OUT MY HEAD AND LOST IT BUT SHE WAS GLAD. I SWEAR DOWN SHE WAS GLAD IT—"

POP! The screen flickered again and the boy fell silent, slumping forwards like a rag doll. We both stared at him in shock. Neither of us dared move at first, but I'm brave about things like this, I know I am. Slow, hesitant, I stepped around the desks, trying to catch a glimpse of the boy's face. I was halfway across the room when something caught the corner of my eye. I stopped, looked around, and flinched back, stumbling into the chairs behind me.

A girl was sat right beside me, her head in her hands, so close I could've reached out and touched her hair.

POP! – and she tipped, not *leant* but *tipped*, back into her chair like a pushed corpse, making me stumble back again with a moan. The girl's eyes were glassy and dead, and her mouth opened, not *moving* just *opened*, and at another *POP!*, her shuddered, tortured voice came through the speakers.

"MISS FAITH HATED ME," she said. "THINGS KEPT GOING MISSING IN CLASS AND MISS FAITH KEPT BLAMING ME. THEN ONE DAY ANOTHER KID'S PHONE TURNED UP IN MY BAG. I DIDN'T TAKE IT. I REALLY DIDN'T, BUT NO ONE WOULD BELIEVE ME."

There was another *POP!* and both me and Miss Faith let out a gasp. At the desk by the control panel, the desk *facing me,* an older man sat with his head in his hands. Suddenly the room stank of alcohol and BO.

POP!

"I DON'T KNOW WHY BECKY FAITH TOOK AGAINST ME," the older man said. "BUT SHE DID. I AM SURE IT WAS HER WHO SPREAD RUMOURS ABOUT MY DRINKING."

"No, I was just ..." Miss Faith moaned. Then she screamed, "*Please!* I'm sorry! I'm *SORRY!*"

Like somebody flicked a switch, the bodies vanished. There was a pause, seconds of dreadful silence and Miss Faith's sobbing breath.

"I'm sorry," she whispered again. "I'm sorry."

She lowered her head and wept, as though it was finished, as though she was forgiven. "I'm so sorry ..."

But I heard the scuttling footsteps again, and I knew. *The elf doesn't forgive. The elf punishes.*

The screen popped and suddenly it blared back on, the light so bright it cast everything else in darkness.

It was showing what looked like an interview – a boy staring straight out at us, at Miss Faith. When he opened his mouth to speak, I recognised his voice. It was the first boy who'd appeared in the chair at the front, the first boy who'd spoken. Only now he looked older, his eyes wired, his hands twitching.

"I TRIED TO GET A JOB, BUT NO ONE WOULD HIRE ME. AND EVERY TIME I SCREWED UP,

I WOULD SEE HER FACE JUST THERE IN THE
BACKGROUND SMILING ABOUT IT AND—"

POP! and the video changed to the girl who'd been
accused of stealing. Her voice grew deeper as she spoke, her
face became gaunt and her eyes hollow.

"NOBODY WOULD TALK TO ME. I LEFT SCHOOL
WHEN I COULD, BUT MY DAD WAS STRICT AND—"

POP! and the video cut to the older man, the teacher.
His eyes were bloodshot and his suit was dirty, and he was
aging rapidly as he spoke – hair turning grey and the bags
under his yellowing eyes deepening into dark grey.

"I'D BEEN A YEAR SOBER. BUT THE STRESS OF IT,
LOSING MY JOB, WAS—"

POP! and the boy grew into a mean, face-tattooed man.

"GOT WITH THE WRONG PEOPLE AND YOU KNOW
WHAT WAS F—"

POP! and the girl became painfully thin, her eyes rolling,
blinking back tears.

"JUST COULDN'T – IT WAS LIKE, MISS FAITH WAS
RIGHT, WANNIT, I WAS—"

POP!

"THAT'S THE IRONY OF IT. IN THE END I WAS
I WAS PR—"

POP!

"PROB—"

POP!

"PROBLEMATIC."

The screen began to pop louder, quicker than it had before.

Each time it flicked between the three interviews, and each time they appeared on the screen they were older, thinner, until finally they . . . *died*.

Yes, died. The old man was first, his yellowing skin turning ashy-white, his eyes glassing and sinking into his skull. His hair fell out, and the flesh of his face greened, then rotted away. But even as luminous bone jutted out through falling skin and flesh, still his mouth kept on moving.

"AS THOUGH BEYOND REDEMPTION, I WAS PROBLEMATIC."

"No," Miss Faith begged but the three of them were practically chanting, all off rhythm with each other like some awful, deranged mantra, as their flesh rotted away.

"PROBLEMATIC, I WAS MESSED, PROBLEMATIC, I WAS A WASTE MAN, PROBLEMATIC, AS THOUGH BEYOND REDEMPTION I WAS—"

"NO!" Miss Faith screamed. She lunged forwards, hands grasping for the control drawer. From nowhere all the corpses lunged out at her and . . . *CRUNCH!* The drawer slammed shut. The voices stopped, the lightboard flicked to a lifeless black. There was a fizz, a flicker, and the classroom lights switched back on. And . . .

"Oh my god," I said. I felt sick.

Miss Faith was staggering back from the console, a strange, animal noise coming from the back of her throat. She lifted her shaking hands in shock, her fingers just *dangling*. The heavy drawer had crushed them, mangled them, into grotesque, bloodied gloves, the skin flayed off to show pulsing tendons and pearly white knuckle. I staggered towards her with sick at the back of my throat, my head throbbing.

That's when I heard it – the *scratching* of claws scurrying away down the corridor.

The elf.

Scrunching my fears, I sprinted across the classroom and out to the hallway, just in time to see the elf darting into the next room, that evil grin on his little face. I was all set to bust in after him, when the door flew open and the elf sped back out. *He doesn't know this school*, I realised. *He doesn't know where to go.*

I sprinted, straight and fast. Tube lights flickered and popped overhead. A tired Christmas tree flew to the floor in front of me. A locker door *PRANG*ed off its hinges, right into my path. Another door burst open ahead of me, and I ignored it, ignored everything, dashing straight for the red fire escape door at the end of the—

"THERE!" I gasped, and as the elf darted out in front of me I dived to grab it – too late and too fast. I missed the elf completely and barrelled into the exit bar, right through the fire door and sprawled face first on to to the cold damp concrete outside. Before I could wonder where the elf was, it was on me. Long claws dug into my neck like razor blades, making me scream with pain. His childlike fingers reached down and squeezed my skull with a bullying strength, and he leant close – so close I could smell his foul, raw-meat breath, and he whispered into my ear some dread incantation I couldn't understand. Faces swam through my mind – hurt faces, crying faces. I saw visions of all the people I'd ever hurt in a terrifying stream of guilty conscience:

> *weight problem leave off fat Simon stinks slapped Faisal asked for it left tramp Krissy crying after Tara wet-the-bed wouldn't leave the changing rooms Alfie till Rose makes herself sick and your why Tyler don't play online any more*

"Hnn*nngh!*" I gasped, my brain clawing to break free from my skull and spill out on to the playground. But the elf did not relent. More sins raced through my tortured mind and *still* those stubby fingers squeezed, squeezed, until my scalp began to lift, and lift . . .

He's flaying my skin . . .

He's scalping me . . .

"Stop!"

It was a commanding cry, from where or who I couldn't tell. Instantly, the squeezing stopped. There was a painful *flurry* of claws across the back of my neck. I heard the *taptaptappaapaparatatatapatatatapapadd* of the elf scuttering away, and in my numb shock I thought I heard footsteps too. I felt the cold of concrete beneath me, felt a dull throbbing pain deep in my skull, and more than anything felt a sharp, stomach-clenching guilt for all the people I'd hurt, the people I'd *bullied*.

And finally, in the distance down the hall, Miss Faith began to scream. She didn't stop until the ambulance came.

—Chapter Twelve—

"...was still screaming when the ambulance came apparently. I mean, thank god Evangeline wasn't hurt herself, although she was – *Edie, would you get your shoes on!* – although she was pretty shook up. Some problem with – *Edie!* – with the power apparently. What's going on with that school, I don't know. How they could have something in there that could do that. I'll be surprised if the poor woman doesn't lose a finger – *Edie, if you don't switch off that TV right now I'm going to...*"

Mum's voice faded down the hall, joined by Edie's whines of protest. I opened my eyes, the dull ache of four fingers and a thumb lingering on my skull like fading bruises.

The guilt though? That was still sharp. That still sickened.

"She's awake!" Dad said gently. He was sat beside my bed, worry in his eyes, his ginger hair and beard messy. I tried to speak, and last night's last sob caught at the back of my dry throat.

"I'm...I—"

"Hey, hey," he soothed, and put a hand on my forehead. "You feel hot, do you have a temperature?"

I swear he asks me that every time something bad happens, right before he reaches for the Calpol, like I'm six. I shook my head.

"How come you're not at work?"

"I said I'd be late," he replied. "But I can take the day off if needs be. We probably won't get much done, they reckon somebody's been sleeping in the Derelicts so the council says we have to waste time cordoning off all the dangerous areas."

"Nah," I said. "I'm fine. I didn't . . ." I felt the scratch of claws on my neck and stuck with the lie. "It was Miss Faith who got hurt, not me."

"It's still a shock!" Dad exclaimed, as Mum appeared in the doorway. "No offence to Miss Faith but I'm *glad* you weren't the one hurt. If you hadn't run to the office when you did . . . You're a bloody hero!"

That made me smile. My dad's OTT, innit. But then a voice at the back of my mind said, *You're no hero. You're a bully.* And my smile faded.

"Wassup?" Dad said, panicking. "Are you hurting? Are you in shock? Do you need Calpol?"

"No, I'm fine, Dad. I—"

"She probably wants some rest, Shay," Mum said quietly. Grateful, I forced a weak smile and Dad relaxed with a chuckle.

"I'll leave you be, eh?" He got up, and added to my Mum, "I might have to work a bit later."

Mum nodded, "Did you say you could get some gaffer tape from work, by the way?" Mum asked.

"Actually," Dad said, "we've just had a load in. I can maybe pinch a roll or two, whaddya need them for?"

"I . . . I don't want to tell you," Mum said. She had a grin on her face, but I'd stopped listening. As Dad got up, I caught sight of something past him, past Mum, to the shelves at the other side of the room, on top of Edie's *Omnidium* where she can't even reach.

It was the elf, in his box. He wasn't finished with me.

". . . just to tape the boxes when we pack the Christmas decorations away."

"*I knew it!*" Dad said, in only *half*-mock horror.

"See this is why I didn't want to tell you."

"Not even Christmas Eve and already you're grinching!"

"I just want to be ready for the new year, ya fool!" Mum said, starting to laugh.

They go through this row every year, like it's a comedy bit. I usually roll my eyes at it, but right then it made me more desperate than ever to keep them safe from harm.

"There's nothing wrong with order—"

"That's what dictators say!"

"You'll be the one wetting the bed if you're missing some tacky bauble next year!"

"My baubles are *gorgeous!*"

Dad realised what he'd said and he and Mum cracked up laughing. Until I blurted out, "Please don't steal the gaffer tape."

They paused, looking at me with surprise.

"Woah, *stealing*?" Dad said. "It's just an extra roll from work, who's gonna miss it?"

Dad shuddup please shuddup it's there it's there it's there . . .

"What's up, Evangeline?" Mum said, looking at me shrewdly.

"It's just . . . it's . . . it's naughty," I said finally. Mum and Dad looked at each other as if they weren't sure whether to laugh or not.

"You're being good," Mum said. "That's good." She wasn't being sarky neither. If anything, she sounded proud. But before she could say any more, Edie stomped in, *furious*.

"*You* told me to switch the telly off and now *you're* taking ages."

"Ey!" Mum and Dad bellowed, and Dad continued telling her off. "Who's 'you'? Have you got your shoes on? Have you got your coat on? You don't just come in here having a go at your mum . . ."

Edie stomped out, Dad hot on her heels. Mum didn't follow. Instead, she came up to the bed. Quietly, she took my phone out of her pocket.

"Seeing as you'll be bored today, and seeing as you've been trying, can I leave this with you and trust that you won't . . .?"

Normally, I'd argue, protest. But phone screens flashed before my eyes – hateful, hurtful things I'd written and been forced to remember the night before.

like shut up happy slapped 2 much acne she's a snake smells of 💩💩💩💩

"No." I said it with venom. Mum nodded, and patted my arm.

"You really did well with Miss Faith last—"

"I'm not a hero, Mum," I interrupted in a low voice. "Please don't say I am. I'm . . . I'm a bully."

There. I'd said it. Mum flinched and that same look of pain flashed across her face, like the word gave her physical hurt. She made to speak, then didn't. Finally, she said something else instead.

"It's Edie's Christmas show tonight. At your school. Won't your Declan and Patrick be there?"

"Yeah," I said. "His kid sister's in theatre club."

"You could come along, hang out with him?" Mum said gently. "Just remind Declan to watch his language, your dad was ready for violence the last time."

I smiled, but that hurt too – my friends. I wondered if Kelsey still hated me, and knew that, yes, of course she did.

"Not tonight I think, Mum," I said. "I just . . ."

I trailed off. Behind me, shadowed in a cold winter sun, the elf still stood, watching. Mum patted my hand and turned to leave.

"Hope you feel better."

"Don't let Dad take that gaffer tape," I blurted out before she left.

She frowned, puzzled. But she nodded and gave a ghost of a smile.

"He'll take this and run with it. We'll have the decs up till March."

I managed to muster a smile back. Finally, Mum turned and left, the sounds of Edie's argument with Dad echoing down the stairs and out the flat. Not a serious argument,

I knew. Not a *sin*, just like taking gaffer tape from work wasn't a *sin*, not in the way Nanna would call something a sin.

. . . the Henki did not care for understanding. The smallest slight, the slightest sin. All deserved its terrible wrath.

An image of Miss Faith's mangled hands flashed through my mind – terror and agony and guilt. Miss Faith had done really bad things. But did the elf really see the difference? Bullying. Stealing gaffer tape. Arguing about the TV. Would everybody be hurt eventually, by the creature that right now stood in its box on top of Edie's *Omnidium*, ever watching, hungry to hurt and bleed and *punish*?

"Not my family," I said to the elf. "No." And I got out of bed.

I was going to the car boot. I was going to find the Strange Owd Woman. I was going to find another copy of *The Blood Texts*, one with the page that said how the Itku Henki were stopped.

I got changed as quick as I could, but because I was kinda skiving off school it took me a while to make myself look older. I didn't have any allowance left either, so instead I took ten pounds out of my parents' change pot and left a note saying I'd taken the money and that I'd explain later. And *yes*, it was more for the elf's benefit than my parents, but either way by the time I was sorted, the morning was almost over. I checked myself in the mirror one last time, hurried to the front door . . . and it opened right in front of me.

"What the . . ." I swore, stepping back – and breathed out.

Standing in the doorway was Elijah. He looked *proper* caught.

"You!" I breathed out. "What you doing here?"

"Me? What are *you* doing here?" said Elijah, in that aggy way people do when they're guilty.

"Uh, *hello*? I'm *ill*, from yesterday?"

"Well, so am I."

"You don't look ill."

"Yeah? You neither."

—Chapter Thirteen—

"So lemme get this – you *still* think this *elf* is—"

"Oh, shut up."

"Chill out, I'm just asking a simple—"

"I mean shut up saying it like that. 'Ew, yew still think this *elf* . . .' I know you don't believe me. I don't know why you came."

We paid our fares to the bus driver – me paying the full adult fare like a school-skipping pro, Elijah thanking him like a pensioner – and went to a seat.

"One . . ." Elijah pointed out. "This is the bus to Stephanie's anyway. *That's* where I'm going. And two – if some mad little doll is on the loose I'm not exactly going to let my kid sister wander round town looking for it—"

"*Shhh!*" I shushed him, looking around. Fortunately, nobody was paying us any attention. "Shut *up* with the kid sister!" I hissed, and Elijah rolled his eyes. I hesitated. "So you do believe me, then?"

"I dunno, Ange . . ." Elijah said, and looked away. "What you're saying, about what happened with Miss Faith, all of that, it's . . . it's too crazy for anyone to make up. But you . . ."

But you've lied a lot before, he *didn't* say. I breathed out, suddenly tired of facing up to all my worst sides. Finally, Elijah sighed.

"So you reckon this elf," he said, "that it's an old spirit that goes around punishing bad people?"

I frowned.

"It's not quite like that. That makes the thing sound like a hero."

"Well . . . yeah, sort of. If Miss Faith was really as bad as all that. She always seemed nice to me."

"Well, *yeah*," I said. "She would do to you – you're the kinda student she'd love, until Stephanie turned you into a big dropout."

Elijah got heated at that right away. He gets really good results and hates the idea that he's not the best person in every room.

"Mum said I should take time off if I was feeling dodge," he snapped. "It's not as simple as that."

"*Exactly*. And *that's* what's messed up about this elf," I insisted. "It views everything in the *worst* possible way, I think. If it wants to, it'll punish you for doing the smallest thing wrong. And c'mon, I hate that Harry, and Miss Faith – I honestly think Miss Faith was a bit evil – but that doesn't mean I think they deserve what happened to them. And *especially* not you—"

"Wait," Elijah said, eyes widening. "You think the elf made the shelves fall on my head?"

I nodded . . . and then something caught my eye. There weren't many passengers on board – an old woman in the seats at the front, reading *That's Not My Santa* to her toddler granddaughter, a mum in a puffer jacket leant on her pushchair in the space in the middle of the bus, a man in yellow overalls in the seat across from us with one of those red Christmas flowers clasped between his gnarled fingers, and . . .

And behind him, in the far corner of the bus, there was the *slightest* flurry of movement. I stared, eyes fixed on that one spot. Nothing happened, for one, two, three . . .

Ttappatappa . . .

Both me and Elijah *whirled* around at the sound. I didn't see any movement that time but Elijah nudged me, his eyes sunken with dread.

I think I saw it, he whispered, so quiet his mouth made no sound.

Where?

Very gently, he nodded directly ahead.

I scanned everything in that direction . . . and froze. There, to the side of the pushchair, the *ghost* of a shadow was peering out just *inches* from the sleeping baby.

I turned back to Elijah.

It's following me, I mouthed. And I suddenly felt very glad my brother was here.

I was so frit by the elf, I didn't answer any of Elijah's questions, no matter how low-key he tried to be. It's a shame, because the bus took *time* to reach the car boot sale, and if I'd told Elijah that's where we were going, he coulda said sooner what he said when we got off; on an empty, run-down street, with empty, run-down warehouses, and an empty, run-down football club opposite.

"Wait, you're going to the *car boot sale*?" Elijah exclaimed. "It's not on today!"

"Er . . . what?"

"It's not a *daily* thing!" he said, annoyed. "What made you think it was?"

"I dunno," I said. "I just . . . I mean, it's always been on when we're there."

"Flip's sake, Evangeline," Elijah said, exasperated. "You've wasted the whole day taking us here! How *stupid* was I to listen, I mean . . . I've gotta message Stephanie, I've—"

Now, being good or not, I was about to a) Remind my brother to *shut it* and *cool it*, because the elf was probably here somewhere too, and b) Teach him just *how* to swear. Then, I noticed a man with a nasty smile, leant up against the locked gates.

"Come to play football?" he said.

"I . . ." I was lost for words. Straight away I didn't like him. Straight away I wanted to run after the bus and bang on the door till the driver let me back on. But I had just enough guts left to bite down on my fears.

"We're looking for a woman," I said. "This weird old woman who sells magazines at the car boot. Bit smelly. Can you help me find her?"

The man looked at me, then at Elijah. Elijah's a square bear at heart, as cool as my mates all *think* he is.

Around properly rough people like this he gets really uncomfortable, and the man with the nasty smile knew it. He nodded at me.

"Just you. I don't let more than one kid in, else they all start *thieving*."

And even before Elijah began to protest, I saw the man's nasty smile widen into an even nastier grin, and I knew he wasn't gonna change his mind.

I would have to go in alone.

———

"It's back here," the man said, and squeezed into the shadows between filthy furniture and sports equipment, his head not *that* low beneath the corrugated ceiling of this small walk-in storage box. It apparently belonged to the football club, this storage box. I didn't care who owned it, of course. I only cared that it was dark, and dirty, and that, ever since I'd gone out of eyeshot of my anxious older brother, I was alone with this creep.

What were you thinking?

"Oi? You coming or what? I don't have all day, y'know."

"Busy bee," I muttered sarcastically. But with a blank stupidity I followed him further inside. The air was cold, and heavy with a mulchy toilet stench. Mouldering dustsheets draped damp over furniture like crap ghosts. A big basket full of toys and dolls made me hesitate, their unblinking eyes glinting dead in the light.

"We let some of the regular booters use this as a storage

unit when they're not coming back for a couple weeks," the man said. "Course, things being as they are, some people just stop coming back."

"Is that what happened with the Strange Owd . . ." I hesitated at the stupid kid's name. "Woman?"

"Her thing was a whole lot weirder," the man said. He'd stopped, and under the faint glow of a swaying lightbulb, I saw that the nasty grin had returned to his face. I paused, suddenly feeling cornered by this shrouded furniture and gloom.

"Her stuff's down here," he said. "You're lucky you came by today, skip lorry's here tomorrow and I'm having a clear out."

Hesitating, I walked closer. What exactly did he mean by *a whole lot weirder*? At his feet, slung across the floor in bin bags, were piles and piles of old magazines. I put on my phone torch and shone the beam over them. Again and again, I saw the title, written in that old-school red font: *The Blood Texts*.

"She left them like this?" I asked. "She was really proud of them before! Where's all those boxes?"

"I burned them," the man said self-righteously. "I don't have time or room here. You leave something, don't expect me to serenade it."

"Where . . . where did she go?"

"Where did she *go*?" Again, that nasty grin. The man glanced out of the storage unit, as if he saw somebody. *Or as if he was checking nobody else was around.* I looked over my shoulder, and my fears increased. The winter light was fading fast.

"Who knows where she went. She was nuts, wannit. Crazy. I used to set her up near the sandwich stand as entertainment. You bought some of her crackpot magazines, did ya?"

"My sister did."

"Well, I hope she didn't pay much. Every month that old biddy turned up with a brand-new set of all those boxes, telling people she was a Strange Owd Woman and how there were deep dark secrets in them. God knows where she got them all from, but they can't have been worth much."

I crouched down over the bin bags, uncomfortably aware of how close this creep was standing. Under the light of my torch, I sifted through the magazines. They were rank; dirt and grime sheened the covers, and the pages felt moist and thin.

"*Issue 32, the Swadlincote Strangler*," I muttered, flicking through. "*Issue 7, The Headless Ghost of the Old Animal Rollercoaster.*"

"She got worse every time, though," the man continued. "Started to say the magazines were poisoning her. Then she said it wasn't the magazines, but it was because she was selling them. ''S'not much to sell your soul for,' I said. '50p for the entire set!' That cracked the guys right up, but she started to get shouty after that. I ended up having to put her at the other end of the car boot sale, away from everybody."

"That's where we saw her," I said. I thought of when Edie had hurried over to the Strange Owd Woman. She'd been standing alone, separated from everyone. I felt a flush of anger at the whole car boot then . . . before flashes of my behaviour came back again.

laughed at him sports day she ran off to the toilets all
red-faced need a bath I said

If I worked here, I wouldn't have been any different to this creep, I realised. I'd have laughed louder than anyone.

". . . must not've been long before she stopped showing up," the creep was still saying. "She left a load of the boxes and her table one day and never came back. I kept the magazines, but I said I'm not using all my space up on pleather boxes. One of the other traders bought the table off me last week an all, as it happens."

I pushed my guilt aside and kept sifting through the magazines. *Issue 23, Neverbelievers, Issue 46, Teke Teke.*

"That's it!" I exclaimed, and pulled the magazine out. I began flicking through it, eager but also dreading that hideous picture of the elf. But before I could find it, another phone torch shone down, right into my eyes.

"Well?" the man barked. "Are you buying it or not?"

"*Buying* it?"

"Yeah. Five pounds for that."

"Five . . . you said they weren't worth anything!"

"Yes, but now they are – to you."

I got to my feet, still holding the magazine. The man leered, and held out his hand for the money.

"That's my bus fare home!"

"*BFH!!!* That's not my problem. Now hurry up, I've got things to do."

"Like what?" I snapped. "Cleaning this scum bucket or swiping Tinder?"

The man took a step closer, all pretence at humour gone.

"You better watch your—"

RRRRRRRRRRip.

At the sandpaper shriek, the lights dimmed and fizzed. When they glowed again, the man's face had lost its menace. His mask had dropped and I stood there, glaring at him, knowing I had nothing to fear. *I'd* done nothing wrong.

"Take the magazine then," he stammered furiously. "Go on, take it – then sod off!"

Just as I was thinking how weird it was, the elf actually *helping* me, I heard the sound of running footsteps, the sound of tripping, and an *oof!* as somebody fell over outside. Taking the magazine, I stepped out of the storage box, my eyes squinting in the cold winter light. Struggling back to his feet, covered in white gravel dust, was Elijah.

"You OK?" he shouted. "I came to see if you were OK!"

—Chapter Fourteen—

It was *cold*. An icy wind tore ribbons off my face and the sparse Christmas lights in the town centre made it colder still. Stuck waiting for the bus, at one point I tried to get *The Blood Texts* out to read but the pages whipped in the wind so fast I thought they'd rip. Finally, we gave up and ducked into a grotty cafe, taking a seat by the window so we'd hopefully see the bus coming. Sat beneath a tatty old advent calendar whose doors had all been opened long ago, I hoped the scowling woman at the till wouldn't bark '*So whaddya want?*' and opened up my new copy of *The Blood Texts*:

```
Itku Henki: The Murdering Moralist!
```

Now I knew that it might just be true, the horrible story about the carpenter who'd captured a spirit and twisted and tortured it into the terrifying elf was grimmer than ever. So it was a *big* relief to turn over and see that the page half-torn from Edie's copy was complete in this one:

Surviving the Itku Henki

With the screams of his neighbours rending the carpenter's pious soul, he looked up to see his captured Henki scampering out towards him, something slick and red dangling from its mouth. As a dreadful hush descended on the grief-stricken crowd, as the corrupted creature opened its mouth and deposited one final mask at the carpenter's feet, a mother's voice pierced the silence, trembling with tears and rage.

"This, this . . . KILLER is yours?"

And as if the tale could not become more tragic, the mother and her neighbours rounded on the carpenter – only to find that this was a dread mistake. For the elf stood between them and the carpenter, and his smile was twisted with a bloodstained glee.

He leapt at them, and very soon the air was torn asunder with the sound of screams and savagery. The awful sobs were choked by sliced flesh. Stains, those the deepest of red, bloomed like roses across the snowy ground. Until at last . . .

"Stop."

It was a piteous cry, the last gasp of a mind cracked into pieces by guilt. It came from the carpenter himself, and to his everlasting horror the Itku Henki gladly heeded his plea, scampering to him with obedient eyes. The carpenter knew now, that he was the Keeper of the Itku Henki, a punishment worse than any the 'elf' could have delivered itself.

You see, ghoulish reader, the Keeper of the Itku Henki can have no friends, no loved ones. They must be isolated from anyone they care about, for given time this sadistic abomination will find a reason to punish the most perfect of souls with knife, claw and the auldest of magicks. And yes, while the Itku Henki can be controlled, or at least restrained, or even **sent to deliver justice** . . . this control is difficult to maintain. It is a curse, to be the Keeper of the Itku Henki, perhaps one that is greater than the elf's own punishments.

That is why, should you ever encounter the elf, you should be good . . . but perhaps not too good. For even worse than being its enemy . . . is being its friend.

"Well, that . . ." Elijah said. "That's no help at all! What's it saying? That *you're* the keeper of the Itku . . . the elf?"

"Don't be dumb," I snapped, before catching myself – *be good, be good, be good.* "I mean, no. The elf attacked me last night, remember? It didn't listen to anything I said before it attacked you. And, let's face it, there's no chance in hell

I've ever been good enough before Friday for a frickin' elf to follow me around, unless somebody sent it to me. I mean, I didn't even *see* it until . . ."

I trailed off, my mind reeling. Elijah peered in, looking closely at me with a worried expression on his face. He began to speak, but I'd stopped listening. Suddenly everything was clear.

Somebody had sent the elf *to* me. Somebody who had every reason for me to change my ways. Somebody who wasn't in trouble all the time, somebody good enough to become the Keeper of the Itku Henki. I knew who that person was, and as I remembered the terror of the last few days – the brutal attack on my brother, on myself, even on Harry and Miss Faith – a white hot fury coursed through my clenching teeth and I dug fingernails into the palms of my hands.

"Ange?" My brother was looking more worried than ever. "Ange, did you hear me?"

"I . . ." I said, blinking.

"You *aren't* a bad person," he repeated earnestly. "You're *not*. You just . . . need more reminding not to mess up, yeah?"

"Uh, yeah," I said distractedly, and pointed out the window. "The bus is here. But did you still wanna go to Stephanie's? Cause I might go to Edie's show."

"At the school?" he said, "That's . . . she'll be happy if you do, she moaned at me for not going. I'll . . . *yeah*, then, if that's OK. I'll go see Stephanie. But – what about the elf?"

I nodded, swallowed . . . and smiled, trying to seem as happy as I could be.

"I think it's gone! I think – I dunno, I think it went off with that creepy man at the car boot. He'd *definitely* need an elf, don't you reckon?"

Elijah stared at me, trying to figure out the lie. Then his phone buzzed, and I knew who it was without even seeing the *Stef bae* picture that lit up the screen.

That's the thing, you see. My brother's a good person – one of the best, I reckon. But nobody's perfect. He *really* wanted to see Stephanie, I knew that. He didn't *quite* believe in the elf, not like I did. And even the best people can believe the words a bad person tells them, if it fits their day right.

I left the cafe and hurried across the road just in time to wave the bus down. Elijah didn't join me. The elf hadn't gone, I knew, but I no longer cared. There was one name I had in my mind, the person who'd sent this elf to me and caused all this harm to me and my family. My plan was dangerous, and *harsh*... and right now, I didn't care.

I was going to see the Keeper of the Itku Henki.

I was going to see *Olivia*.

— Chapter Fifteen —

After three knackering days of crappy goodness, rage felt *great.* I got on the bus, squashed myself a seat between this tutting old bag and a young dad wearing his tragic baby sack like he was the Virgin Mary, and I urged the traffic forwards with a steady silent stream of foul language. It made no difference; we *crawled* along, swaying back and forth, the bus's motor rumbling on petrol then *whooshing* us on electric. Somebody wanted to get on between stops and started slamming the door – *BLAM BLAM* – when the driver ignored them, and while everybody else looked down I stared at them both, eager to see a fight break out. This was me, I knew, the real me. The elf could do what he wanted, I would never be anything but a bully, a thug, a *bitch.* No more lying, 'cept to everybody else but me.

Finally, the man outside gave up and stormed off. Disappointed, I pulled my bag up on to my lap – earning a huff off new-dad when I knocked his dumb polka-dot nappy sacks over – and took my phone out. There was a message off Mum in her old school txt spk.

hope ur ok hun you comin edies show? rice n fritters n fridge if not.

And only one message from my friends, from Declan.

WTF Ange. Is it true?

What did that even mean? I began writing a message back – wtf do you mean wtf? – then stopped bothering. Whatever he meant, *Olivia* had done this. She was at the Christmas show, it was why I was going, but screaming at her there wasn't going to cut it, especially not with the elf around. I'd have to be smarter than that, and meaner. And then I remembered the photograph.

And she's at the Christmas show.

Quickly, I swiped to the Trash folder in my photos. There it was – Olivia falling back, legs splayed out, face ugly with surprise. It had been such a big decision to delete it, like choosing to be good. Now I was undoing that.

She's at the Christmas show. It's too perfect.

Eyes cold, I dragged my rucksack on to my lap, this time to get my make-up mirror. It was *still* the Christmas show, even if it was gonna be my last. Course, I knocked over new-dad's changing bag on purpose this time.

"It's not the baby Jesus, you know," I said when he huffed again. "And you didn't give birth to it neither. You can get over yourself."

God it was good to be back.

— Chapter Sixteen —

It had begun to rain by the time I walked through the school gates. I pushed through the main doors only to be smacked by skin-prickling heat and a shouting crowd – grinning parents with plastic cups and Santa hats, teenagers cringing at their jokes, younger kids busting lungs with excitement. Gritting my teeth, I waded through it, aiming for the backstage left doors at the end of the corridor while keeping eyes peeled for Edie or my parents. That's when I noticed that eyes everywhere were flicking up at me like kicked-up leaves.

It wasn't from any of the adults, it was from the kids – stares, nudges, whispers. The stares were *angry*, I realised, filled with dislike. I saw Edie's friend Meera shoot me a dirty look, strode up to ask just what her problem was . . . when her friend turned around and I froze. It was Edie.

"What are you doing here?" she said, and, before I had time to answer, "Did you really attack Miss Faith?"

"*What?!*" I blurted out. But Edie's friend Meera stepped forwards, her face suddenly twisted with rage.

"She was my *favourite teacher*!" she hissed, and I was so stunned by the bizarre accusation that I stepped backwards, bumping into some kids from the year above. One of them *flinched* like I was about to attack her, while her clingy boyfriend shoved me away.

"Don't even think about touching her," he said, one arm wrapped protectively around her neck. "Y'get me?"

"Evangeline," Edie said, but I stumbled away, desperate to escape this hostile crowd. That's when I saw Mum and Dad walking in.

"'k sakes!" I muttered. There was nowhere else to go. I shoved left through the crowd and ducked into the girls' toilets, glancing back before the door closed behind me to see Edie pointing in my direction, mouthing *Evangeline?* to Mum. Her gaze swept towards me like a searchlight beam and I raced to the nearest cubicle to hide.

What. The. Actual . . . How did people think I had attacked Miss Faith? I sat on the lid of the toilet, caught between tears and fury. *Everything* that could go wrong had gone wrong. My life was in ruins. I couldn't see any way out. And just when things couldn't get any worse, the toilet door opened to harsh, cruel voices. The voices belonged to my ex-best friends.

" . . . nobody knows, but she's always been weird. Once, I was round her house and her brother – ohmygod he's fit – he started ragging on her about how she'd left all her belly button fluff on the side of the bath!"

"Ew!" That was Emma.

"I know. She went mental. It was honestly kinda *toxic*. Which, when I heard about Miss Faith, it made me wonder what happened, you know?"

"You think she attacked her, then?" That was a new voice. It took a moment for me to twig which voice it was, then I realised – it was Sophie from my English class, one of the Cringes. *She's trying to get in the crew.*

"You think she attacked her then?" Kelsey said, imitating Sophie's posh voice, and then laughed. "Just kidding. But yeah, I do. She's never been right in the head. I'm just saying, we should watch our—"

Just then, at the worst possible time, my phone vibrated with a call – not loud, but loud enough. The girls stopped talking abruptly, and there was a dreadful pause.

"Who's that?" Kelsey said, her voice harsh. I froze, staring dumbly down at my phone. There was a missed call from Mum, and to make matters worse the phone vibrated again with a message from her.

Are u here?!

BANG! the cubicle door rattled right near my head.

"Oi," Kelsey said, her voice filled with malice. "Who's nosey?" Still I didn't answer. The door *pounded* again, and I thought she was going to break it . . . when the headteacher's voice echoed through the tinny school speakers.

"Parents and students, festive greetings. Our Christmas extravaganza is about to begin, would you kindly make your way to the school hall and take your seats!"

"I'd better go," Sophie sighed, *trying* to sound annoyed.

"Ohhh, you're *in* the show!" Kelsey said, amusement in her voice. "I'm just here with Dec – his kid sister's in it. I'd forgotten anyone *our* age even did it."

"Ugh, well I wouldn't have to if Pik-Sen wasn't always putting my name in," Sophie said quickly as the toilet door opened and they all filed out. "She really gets on my nerves. Anyway, what do you think Evangeline *did*?"

The door closed again, and I was left sitting alone. Was Kelsey the one spreading rumours then? She def wasn't helping things either way, and as cold as I'd always known she'd been, I still felt a stab of betrayal, so sharp that I took out my phone and wrote a message to Declan, just to mess with her head:

I Miss You

But before I could send it, the headteacher blared through the speakers again and I stuffed my phone in my pocket without sending.

"One minute warning, all you parents and siblings!"

It was a reminder to me. This was *Olivia's* doing, all of it. *She'd* asked for this. It was *her* night.

I peered out to the hallway. It was empty, save for the last parents entering the auditorium, and a geeky Year Seven kid holding the door open for them. I raced past them for the backstage left door at the end of the corridor, peered through the glass . . . and saw with dismay that it was *busy*. Even worse, Mr French, the Drama teacher, was standing right in the middle. There was no way he'd let me through.

"Erm," the Year Seven geek said nervously behind me.

"If you'd like to be seated, the auditorium is *this* way."

"Slow your roll, Ticketmaster," I snapped. "I'm talent."

Just as Mr French looked up, I turned and hurried back up the corridor. The backstage right door is always quieter but to get there I'd have to go through the canteen, which is connected to the auditorium by these massive folding doors. My adrenaline was up now and rather than tiptoe through, I shoved the swinging canteen doors open with such force that they bounced off a table with a loud clatter, sending me tripping like a goof-troop. Luckily, the sound was drowned out by the shrieking sounds of Edie's theatre club murdering the opening carol, and I hurried on through the canteen to the corridor on the other end.

"Evangeline?"

I was halfway along the corridor, the backstage right door just ahead of me, when a familiar voice called softly back from inside the canteen.

"Evangeline?" It was Olivia.

Not now. I don't want to see you now, I thought, and hurried on.

"Evangeline, you've . . . you dropped your phone."

I felt my pockets and swore – it must've dropped out when I bowled through the doors. With no other choice, I hurried back to the canteen, only to see *Olivia*, the one person I *didn't* want to see, standing in front of me with my phone in her hand and a nervous smile on her face.

"Thanks," I said, but I couldn't smile back. I didn't have time for pity right now. I looked past her, at the tinselled tables I'd barged the door into. They were stacked with paper cups filled with cheap fizzy pop. Several cups on the end by the door had been knocked over, neon-bright orange liquid trickling sticky and slow off the table's edge. *Me*, I thought. *I did that.* And kicked myself for feeling guilty.

She asked for this. She ruined your life.

"I did say my job was *back*stage," she said wryly. Great, she wasn't even being *annoying*. This was messing up my plan, slowing me down, making me doubt myself.

"You're still getting the credit for it though," I said flatly. She nodded, and for a second her face dropped into a weird look of guilt and fear, before she handed my phone over, my home screen brightening at the movement.

"Thanks," I said. "I've got to go."

"No problem," Olivia said. That nervous smile again, and she turned back to the tables, saying nothing like of *course* I should leave while she cleaned up the mess I'd made. I thought of saying more, but I knew somehow that if I did, the bad feeling in my stomach would take over and I wouldn't be able to go through with my revenge. *She did this*, I thought desperately. *She RUINED YOUR LIFE!*

And with that comforting excuse, I turned around and hurried out, left down the corridor to the backstage right door, my feet pounding a rhythm *be good be good be good be—* before I shut up my head. I pulled open the door and instantly was bombarded by the screech of Edie's mic'd up choir. But it was at least quieter here, just two conversations; a hushed argument between three spotty older boys, and the excited whispers of two girls from my year.

"... no! *You* pause, then I make the joke, *then* we sing the song!"

"... Uh, Soph, these stupid clips keep coming undone – I swear my wings are going to fall off halfway through ..."

"Handles for forks, Nicholas! We can't change the wording, that's the joke!"

"... yeah, but this is the best part. See Kelsey told me that Evangeline Clark went mad and—"

"Went mad and what, Sophie?" I said. Sophie stopped, scared. I smiled sweetly at her, my fists at my sides. Her friend, Pik-Sen, stood behind her, not looking at her wing clips any more.

"Evangeline!" Sophie said, uncertainly. "You ... what's up?"

"Just got a thing to sort out," I said, and turned to Pik-Sen. "You know she said you get on her nerves, don' cha?"

Sophie blinked. Her mouth did a smirk – like *here's the mental case I warned you about!* – but her eyes couldn't quite shake their fear and she didn't argue with me. I strode on past her and through the darkened backstage area. At the very back, behind a grey door, was the control room. I hurried over, my phone in hand, and opened the door ... only to be swallowed up by a cinnamon vape fog. Patrick was leant back, playing with his laptop – until he saw me and damn near coughed out his chair.

"Ange!" he exclaimed, and frowned. "I thought you were feds!"

"You mean Mister French," I said dryly, although the

way his eyes were shining from whatever was in his vape, he might actually have thought the police were chasing him.

"What are you doing here?"

"Last minute add," I said, and held up my phone. "Apparently, Olivia wants to be part of the sketch show now."

Even behind that permanent fug, Patrick's eyes frowned at this. I had to admit, it sounded far-fetched.

"Olivia? Why isn't she here then?"

"She's just sorting out the drinks," I lied. "She's in a rush, that's why she wanted me to do it."

Still, he frowned. It was a weak reason. Desperate, I stretched for another lie.

"It's coming just after the end of their act. Fork Handles or something?"

Patrick raised his eyebrows.

"The *Bobby Dazzlers*, those boys from the year above? One of them has been trying to chat Olivia up all through rehearsals . . ."

I shrugged, like *what can I say?*

"They want to add a picture at the end of that sketch. Here."

Unlocking my phone, I swiped across to the terrible image of Olivia and handed him the phone.

Olivia, you asked for this.

-Chapter Seventeen-

Patrick whistled.

"She really wants to put this on there? She's a total rabbit normally."

I shrugged. My head was suddenly *pounding* – five points on my skull from where the elf's fingers had grabbed on to my head. Shameful memories and *pushed her tripped him laughed* guilt was cutting into my rage.

But my dad always says, *in for a penny . . .*

"We're friends now, innit," I said with a horrible false lightness. "She's more chill."

"Well, good, but . . ." Patrick stared at the image, and shook his head. "This is *butters*. Are you sure she won't mind this?"

"You can ask her!" I said, and a growing part of me silently begged him to *Please! Please ask her, please refuse, please get me out of this!* "She's just putting all the drinks on the table for the interval. But she said it'd work at the end of that fork handles joke. Uh . . . *handles for forks*?"

A sharper look cut through Patrick's usually hazy

expression, and he studied me. I shrugged awkwardly back, wearing the most innocent look I could muster.

"You know," he said, "I'm glad you're friends with Olivia now. I didn't . . . I didn't really like when you used to mess with her. I shoulda . . . I shoulda said something. But it's good you're friends now."

"Yeah, I wanted to change," I said quietly. Weirdly enough, I didn't want to properly lie to him. "It's pissed Kelsey off."

Patrick grunted, air-dropping the image off my phone on to his laptop. It appeared on the screen, all blown up. Olivia falling back, that mortifying look on her face, globules of gravy spattered up her face and nostrils. Part of me had the sudden urge to tell Patrick to cancel, to say the whole thing was a joke. Then I thought of Elijah lying there, blood trickling from his skull, of slipping off the kitchen sideboard after I'd deleted this photo. I thought of all the harm Olivia had put me in.

"Kelse needs to chill," Patrick said finally. "But if she can't get over it . . . y'know, you've still got friends, Ange."

Then he pressed a couple of shortcut keys and the image disappeared into the timeline on his editing software.

"Done."

"Thanks, Patrick," I said, forcing a smile. It was my big moment, my big revenge . . . and I felt like I'd just made a terrible, *awful*, mistake.

Feeling sick, I walked out of the choking wet vape fog, shut the door behind me and stumbled back through backstage, ignoring everyone. The exit doors felt heavy and

I felt weak, guilt eating me like bleach with every step. I've done some bad things – really *bad* things – but this felt like the worst, the gift that would keep giving. Worst possible outcomes spun through my head – people snapping the image and sharing it, Olivia finally breaking under the shame and the ridicule she'd get. And my punishment, the elf. If I hadn't deserved him before, I deserved him now. Would he hurt my family too?

I took the long way back, along the back corridor, and was almost at the exit when Mum came out of the toilets further down. She clocked me once ... then stopped, stunned.

"'Ange?!" she exclaimed.

I didn't want to talk right then. I hurried on, barging through the main door and out to the front yard.

"Ange!" Mum called after me. "Evangeline, stop! STOP!"

I was at the bottom step when she grabbed my arm. Finally, I turned to look up at her.

"What's going on?" she said. "Edie said she saw you but I said that was impossible. What are you doing here?"

"Nothing," I said, my voice strangled. Concern flooded Mum's face, then sadness. I couldn't meet her eyes, like they *hurt*.

"I thought we were getting out of this,"

"I know," I said. "And I'm so sorry, Mum. I'm *so* sorry. I know you got bullied and I know that makes you hate me and—"

"What?" she said, startled.

I looked down at my feet, guilt pouring out of me, fury

at my own stupid temper and stupid behaviour.

"I know you were bullied at school," I said. "I can see it on your face. It must be so gutting to see, and I don't . . . I don't know why I do these things but I—"

"Evangeline," Mum said.

I looked up.

"Evangeline . . . I was the *bully*."

For a long time we just stood there, staring at each other. Part of me felt a shameful relief. Part of me felt revulsion.

"There was a girl at my school," Mum said, and cleared her throat. "And she was different. In fact, she probably wasn't, but we were all idiots and we were all scared and so we made her different, just so we felt more alike. I don't . . . Anyway," she continued, clearing her throat again. "We picked on this girl. We were horrible. Her friends were scared too – more scared of us than we were – and because they were weak, because we were all weak, we turned them against this girl, got them to join in with our, our . . ."

"What did you do to her?" I asked. Mum started to say something . . . "We . . ."

Then she shook her head.

"We bullied her. Until she was all alone – until she had no confidence, no friends, nothing left that could be considered good in her life. We stripped it all away, until . . ."

"What happened?" I asked, dreading the answer. But Mum shook her head.

"She left the school in the end," she said eventually. "Thank god. If she hadn't . . . Of course, at the time *we* all laughed, said she'd get the same trouble at the next school, because she asked for it."

"Did she?" I asked finally, but Mum looked at me with fury and tears in her eyes . . . and she *never* cries.

"*Nobody* asks for what we did," she muttered. "*Nobody* does."

Mum looked away and wiped her eyes delicately with a finger.

"Did you ever see her again?" I asked, and she nodded.

"Once. Years later. I was at the shops, and she was . . . suddenly just there. I wish I could say I'd had this building guilt about what we did, but it wasn't like that. It was more like . . . it just hit me *then*, like," she struck her stomach. "Like a punch, and *ohh* . . ."

"Did you say something?"

"I called out her name before I knew what I was doing. She saw me, and she . . . she sort of jerked back. Like I was a big spider. I stood there for ages, and I wanted to say sorry so much. But she just blinked and hurried off."

"You should find her," I said. My voice was thick, my nose was suddenly blocked. Mum shook her head.

"She didn't want to see me. And I don't have the right any more. Doing that – doing what I did . . . She doesn't want to see me ever again. All I can do is think about it and feel bad. And that feeling never goes away. Ever. You don't lose it, Evangeline. You're not allowed to."

I stared at her, speechless and horribly sad. Finally, Mum swallowed, and squeezed my hand.

"But you can try to be good. If you're lucky, you'll

get surrounded by people who make you want to be good. And if you get any chance . . . any chance at all to undo a bad thing you've done to Olivia, then you should jump at it. Because it's those missed chances that keep me up at night."

I stared at her, stunned. Then Mum gave me a half-smile and patted my arm. I leant in and hugged her, the first time I've hugged her in ages. She gave a strange, annoyed look, and for a really clear moment I knew that she felt guilt for having a daughter who gave her a hug, after the way she'd treated that girl at her school. Then, with a nod, blinking furiously, she turned and hurried back inside, up the steps and through the door to the school show.

For a long while, I just stood there. The school loomed over me, a window of light surrounded by dark and cold. I looked further around, to the Derelicts, where building site fencing creaked in the wind.

"I've got to get that photograph down," I said, and started back up the steps towards the main door. That's when—

BLAM! Something hard struck me across the side of the head and I tumbled down the steps, every cold corner jabbing bruises into my body until I came to a stop on the concrete driveway. Dazed, terrified, I scrabbled to my feet, gasping out snot and spit as I whirled around looking for the elf. Then I stopped, dead still.

"Miss you," Kelsey said. "*MISS YOU?!*"

– Chapter Eighteen –

"Get up," Kelsey snarled. "Come on, get up."

"I didn't send that text," I said. "Kelsey, I can't do this right now I—"

BLAM! Kelsey kicked me in the side and I fell down with a whimper.

"*I didn't send that text*," she mimicked. "Funny how you know what I'm talking about then." Another girl laughed, a laugh I recognised, and I lifted my head. On one side of Kelsey was another *ex*-friend, Emma. To the other side, was Sophie the Cringe.

"You were right, Soph," Kelsey said. "I didn't think she'd be so *thick* as to DM my boyfriend *and* show up to the school on the same night."

Sophie gave a weak laugh. But she looked freaked out. This was deeper than she'd planned for.

"Should we go back inside?" she said.

"Kelsey," I begged. "This is a bad idea, you don't know what will happen."

"What I know," Kelsey snarled, "is that you've been

sending messages to Declan, telling him you'll get with him."

"What?!" I said. "I didn't, Kelsey. Who told you I—"

BLAM! Kelsey kicked me again and I fell forwards with a cry, a horrible pain to my ribs and no air in my lungs. Shaking, struggling up to my hands and knees, I saw the school entrance lights flicker, all around us.

"Kel . . . *Kelse*," I said through deep, trembling gasps. "I know . . . we've fallen out. But *please*, as . . . a friend . . . you *need* to run."

I let my head hang again, crouched forwards with my hands splayed on the freezing concrete in front of me like a yoga stretch. There was a pause, long enough for me to remember how to breathe again. And Kelsey stepped forwards, digging the full weight of one shoe into the back of my hand.

"No, Kelsey. No," I begged. She crouched low, so low that her face was near mine, and whispered into my ear.

"You don't have any friends, Ange."

BrrrrrrrRRRIPP!

It came from my right, those quick scuttling steps, rapid and light, and Kelsey rose, mercifully stepping back off my hand in surprise. I looked up, my senses sharpened with pain, and heard a horrible *slicing* sound rush past Sophie. There was a pause, and then Sophie let out a cry.

"What?" Kelsey snarled, fear as well as rage in her voice.

"Ohmygo . . . *god* . . ." Sophie said, her wannabe rude voice petering out as she looked down at her legs, where a steady stream of blood trickled to a *dripdripdrip* on the concrete floor. With her mouth part-open in shock, Sophie twisted her leg around and I saw a large, dangling square of skin, peeled back from each calf. Staggering back, Sophie began to gulp; bizarre, hyperventilating swallows of freezing air.

"What did you do, you psycho?" Kelsey said, her voice hard. She was talking to me.

"Kelsey, I didn't—"

"WHAT DID YOU DO?!"

It had been the last thing Miss Faith had said too. There was another *RRRRRIP!* and something bounded towards us out of the dark, flying past Emma with that same, horrible *slicing* sound.

"Kelse," Emma said in a high, trembling voice. She lifted her shaking arms to reveal two, long, bloody bracelets of skin hanging from the wrist.

This couldn't be any more messed up. A shameful part of me felt a glint of triumph, a fury that *wanted* them to be attacked. Right then, I *hated* my friends. But then Emma fell to her knees, that girl I used to practise dance moves with, the girl I'd laughed with until we'd snorted, and then laughed some more. And as she *screamed* out a sob, all of that triumph vanished. I didn't want this to happen to my friends.

"Kelsey," I whispered. Kelsey whipped back around to look back at me. "You have to run."

At that, I launched up to my feet like a track athlete, barging Kelsey back, and burst forwards, sprinting as fast as I could back up the school steps. Despite all the turmoil of the past minutes, the elf's attack and the horror of seeing my former friends savagely attacked had only made one thing clearer – *I had to get rid of that photo.*

I burst through the main doors, just as laughter echoed out from the auditorium, and raced down the hallway towards backstage left, my shoe soles slapping the floor so loud it made the Ticketmaster kid flinch away from the glass – and flinch again at the sight of me.

"You can't—" he began.

"*Shut* up," I spat, and raced past him to backstage left which was . . . locked.

"I tried to say it before!" Ticketmaster whined. "Mr French only left the other one open, I thought you'd already . . ."

Before he could finish, the school front doors SLAMMED open and Kelsey stepped in.

"You're not getting away that easily," she spat, and strode towards me. "*Get here.*"

"Kelse," I said quietly, half-begging. "You know I didn't do that. You know there's something else here—"

"Don't care," she said, and repeated it, louder and more threatening. "I *don't care.*" She really *didn't* care, I realised with horror. It was as if rage had clouded every sensible thought except for the need to cause me pain, to punish me. Uncertain, I stepped towards the hall . . . and the door opened.

"What the *devil* is going on out here?" a voice asked in outraged whisper. It was Miss Acres. She looked to Kelsey, then to me. "Evangeline, what are you . . ."

I didn't hear what she had to say as I forced myself past her into the hall. Nor did I hear the murmurs from the audience, the "*Ange?*" whispered in the dark from my mortified mum or dad, though I *know* one of them woulda said it. I didn't hear Miss Acres repeating her questions, going from stern to concerned. I didn't hear the scattering steps of the elf and I didn't hear the last shouted threats from Kelsey, though I knew from the way the other teachers turned their frowns from me to the doors that she'd shouted *something*.

I didn't hear any of this because all I heard were the two older geeky boys stood on stage, one of them in a flat cap and the other one in old-time breeches. They were carrying out a sketch, and they were enjoying themselves so much that even with all the disturbance I'd caused they were carrying on with it,

"Four candles?"

"Nah! Fork handles. As in handles, for forks."

That's the cue that's the cue that's the . . .

And there it was. There wasn't a sound to announce it. Why would there be, when I hadn't tricked Patrick into adding one? But it was a full-size photograph, that hadn't been tested on the screen like the comedy set background had and so was *painfully* bright – so bright that people shielded their eyes with a wince before dropping them in complete astonishment.

The air went still.

There, up on screen was . . .

"What?" said Olivia from the back. I turned and saw her standing by the folding doors to the canteen, a horrible, *heartbreaking* dismay on her face.

"Olivia," I said. "I'm so sorry."

And with a *SLAM!* all the lights went out.

— Chapter Nineteen —

The chaos was instant. Kids screamed – some with genuine terror, some because they thought it was funny to scream. Chairs scraped quickly back, phone torch beams flickered on, flitted across terrified faces . . . and dissolved like tissue paper in a flood of darkness. I heard the quietest scuttling of claws across the ceiling high above us all and, either because of this or the choking darkness, the parents – who at first stayed calm – spoke louder and more urgently, a muttering panic that spread like COVID across the room.

It was in here, I knew. *It was in here and it was here for me.*

"CASSIE!" one of the dads called out at last. "CASSIE, WHERE ARE YA BABE?"

This sparked off a few more parents calling out. Before long, kids got in on the act as well.

"Mum! Mum, are you there? Mum, where—"

"Mummy!!!"

"Over here, Mya. Is that—"

"Mummy! Mumsy Wumsy!"

More people started getting to their feet. The room got

louder, and hotter, air and noise suffocating me. Blindly, I stumbled back the way I came, groping out for the hallway door, but there was already a crowd of people struggling to get out, led by the same Loud Dad who'd shouted first of all. He shouted again now.

"CASSIE, DON'T WORRY BABE! CASSIE, DON'T WORRY BABE. FOLLOW MY VOICE!"

"Calm down, pal," another dad said. "Let's not have a baby, shall we?"

"DON'T YOU TELL ME TO CALM DOWN, YER PRI—"

That horrible *slicing* sound raced through the air around me. Horribly, I felt several drops of wet on my face . . . and Loud Dad screamed. Fizzing phone torches shone meekly from all around me, a second's illumination that glowed on Loud Dad as he stumbled, blood trickling from his face.

It would've been so much better had nobody seen that. Instantly, the panic *accelerated*. Footsteps sped up behind me, chairs clattered to the floor, and I was hit in the back first by one kid who tripped and fell into me, then by a whole crowd of people.

"There's blood here!" somebody screamed. "It's blood, it's blood! We're being attacked!"

"*OK!*" Miss Acres shouted. "*OK, we need to calm d—*"

If anyone could've calmed the room it was her, but it was too late for that. As a single, selfish mass, the entire crowd swayed towards the door, cutting Miss Acres off and, from the sound of it, knocking her to the floor in the process. I was powerless to escape, but in a stroke of good luck the crowd surged forwards and I was spat like vomit back out to the corridor.

The lights here were clinging dimly on, and with the pale moonlight that dribbled through snow-sprayed windows and tinselled entrance doors, I could see well enough to break away from the pouring, manic crowd and look back to search for my parents. What I saw instead was awful. The crowd inside the auditorium had become a bottleneck – a violent mob, spewing out shouts of anger, cruel laughter, and fear.

"Mum, help!"

"Who's doing it? Somebody grab 'em and we'll—"

"It's terrorists! I said this, and nobody listened—"

"Get off me, *get off me*!"

Grim-faced teenagers were shoving blindly forwards – Omar from Year 10 elbowing left and right, Smiffy in the year below me straight kicking *off* at a terrified younger kid. It wasn't just the kids either – Gold-digger nearly reached the door, only to be yanked back by the scruff of his neck by a tight-lipped woman who pushed her daughter ahead of him. Somewhere Miss Acres let out a shriek, then the crowd surged again and that shriek was cut violently short. People were turning into animals, losing every bit of goodness in their sheer desperate need to *escape*. It was hell.

And heaven for the elf. I could see it working its way through the bottlenecked crowd that was pushing its frantic way to the doors. Smiffy got his first, jerking forwards as though somebody had kicked his spine, eyes bulging before he *screeched* with agony. The mum attacking Gold-digger got hers next, letting go of Gold-digger's shirt like he'd shocked her, holding up dripping hands before she began to violently shudder. By the time Omar fell brutally to the floor, I had to look away.

The only way they'll escape is with the lights on.

The only way they'll escape is with the elf gone.

"Hey!" I shouted. "Hey, Itsy Bitsy, Henki Denki, whatever your name is! I'm here if you're going to get me, you dirtbag freak. Don't get them, get *me*!"

I paused for a moment, listening out . . . but nothing changed.

"*Oi!*" I shouted again. "Don't you wanna catch me? Don't you wanna punish me?"

"Yes," another voice hissed spittle into my face, and my heart sank. I turned to see Kelsey standing there, hands clenched into fists.

"Please, Kelse," I begged. "Please, not now. *Please.*"

But she's different to me, Kelsey. My ex-best friend had something . . . missing. My mouth going dry, I stepped back, but it was too late. Kelsey slammed out one hand like a shot and gripped my hair, pulling me down with an evil, *tearing* strength. As I groaned with pain, she pulled back her other fist, an inhuman leer on her face, and . . .

The corridor lights gave up at last.

BrrrrrrrRRRIPP!

It happened in stop motion – a blur of blood and shadows

under the flicker of a hundred failing phone torches. Kelsey was gripping me one moment and the next she was writhing on the floor under the elf's frenzied attack. I can't bring myself to remember those images, and at the same time I can't escape them. They're punctuated with those terrible *slicing* sounds, with Kelsey's pig-like squeals and the screams of everyone around her. Until one last voice rose above the terror, loud and clear.

"STOP! PLEASE, *PLEASE* STOP!"

And mercifully, the elf did.

Kelsey collapsed to the floor, barely recognisable. The mob fell into stunned silence. In the distance, I heard the sobs of people outside the building and inside the hall. Finally, my dad's tremulous voice came from the darkened auditorium, quiet and afraid.

"Ange? Are you all right, love? Ange?"

"Dad," I said, fighting back a sob. "Dad, is everyone all right? Where's Mum, where's Edie and Elij—"

That's when I saw her, the person whose voice had made the elf stop. She was stood shaking by the front doors, her pale unhappy face pinched in the moonlight.

"Olivia," I croaked. "Olivia, you have to—"

But before I could say another word, Olivia turned and ran outside.

"We're all here, Ange," Mum began. "We're all right—"

But before *she* could finish, I was running for the exit too.

– Chapter Twenty –

The rain had turned to hail, frozen bullets that peppered at my face. The icy breath hurt my lungs like swallowed blades, and every direction promised trouble – from the sirens racing down the streets ahead, the sobbing survivors of that brutal attack spilling out from the school corridors behind me, and the abandoned, rat-infested Derelicts to my right ...

The Derelicts ...

Suddenly, something occurred to me. Before I suspected Olivia had anything to do with the elf, I'd figured that the Derelicts had been his home, that my dad had accidentally unearthed it while ripping out a fireplace. Now I knew different, that place suddenly seemed to explain more, and all the strange moments with her flashed before my eyes.

Plastic shoes on a Saturday ...

"Nobody has the number for her parents – none of the *Whatsapp groups have her ...*"

Research her family tree, but the one time I'd asked she'd been all weird and vague ...

Reeks of BO – like, have a shower please . . ."They reckon somebody's been sleeping in the Derelicts, so . . ."

I'd already started to run forwards when I saw her; the figure of a girl climbing the fence in the dark. Olivia, whose family nobody knew, whose history nobody had bothered to ask for. The girl who smelt sometimes, the girl who wore plastic school shoes on a Saturday. The girl who couldn't not sound like a swot, the sad girl we called a sad act. The girl whose life I'd made even *more* miserable than it was already.

She's been living in the Derelicts, I thought. *She's homeless.*

And feeling wicked, feeling damned, I raced on after her with no idea what to do when I caught up.

The Derelicts are creepy enough in the daytime, but at night . . . they were *terrifying*. The floors in the buildings were dirty concrete and creaking wooden boards. The walls were mouldering plaster and graffiti – hate-filled messages threatening violence scrawled ten feet high. Every corner was pitch black; every void flurried with movement in the corner of my eye. I couldn't hear the elf, not yet, but I knew I didn't have long.

"Olivia!" I called. Unsurprisingly, she didn't answer. I raced past taped-off rooms, past ripped-down walls and ripped-up floors . . . then skidded to a stop. I was being stupid. Olivia would never have stayed *here*, else Dad or one of his workmates would've found her straight away. She would be at the far end, where work hadn't even begun yet.

I raced out through a smashed-up front door and out to the street. For all the times I'd climbed through the gap in the school fence, I'd never gone all the way through the Derelicts to the other side. The houses opposite weren't as run down as these, but they weren't far off. A dog barked savagely at me from behind a barbed wire fence, while some older boys sat smoking on a wall shouted something I couldn't make out. I didn't hang around to say 'pardon' neither, running across cracked tarmac and loose paving until I reached the last abandoned house and caught a glimpse of torchlight in the top-left window. Olivia was there, I was sure of it.

The front door seemed locked until I shoulder barged it and it budged. Another shove and it flew open, sending a folded piece of card that must've wedged it in fluttering to the floor. The hall was dark and decayed but somebody upstairs was running about, slamming, moving things.

"Olivia!" I called again. No response, but the banging suddenly stopped. I switched on my phone torch and raced up the stairs, nearly twisting my ankle at a missing step five up, and flinched back at the top step, a moan escaping my throat as a *massive* rat raced across my trainer and down the hallway! The bedroom door at the end of the landing was ajar, and as I ran for it the words just spilt out of my mouth.

"Olivia, I'm sorry I'm sorry I'm . . ."

The room was empty, but somebody had been in here. The streetlight spilt in through a window, on to an air mattress on the floor and to an open holdall. It was grim, her life, more grim than I would ever have possibly imagined. I stood and stared. And when her voice spoke behind me, I wasn't surprised with what she said.

"You said you deleted that picture."

I turned.

"Olivia, I'm sorry—"

"You screwed everything up. You ruined my life, and then you screwed everything up."

I stared. Olivia was angry, the first time I'd seen her *properly* angry, fists bunched, voice dancing angry.

"I had it all planned out. I was going to escape. And you couldn't not be a bitch for five minutes, could you?"

She took a step towards me and I couldn't help myself, I stepped back, further into the room. Olivia noticed, smiled, fury in her glittering eyes. She gave a nod to the room.

"Like my house?"

"Olivia, I'm—"

"Does it explain the BO?"

"I shouldn't have said that . . ."

"Course, I've got a family, my dad, somewhere. He was a good dad – probably he's still looking for me. I was a good daughter. I was really good, not something I would ever have said, but I was. Not like you. I was a good person when I didn't have to be. Then that *monster* came. I don't know who'd brought it, I just know that it turned up one day. I was kind to it, and it didn't leave. But when other people near me did bad things, it would *attack*. It's like a curse, this elf. It liked me, looked after me, and I really didn't want it to. And as time went on, it began to attack the people I cared about. When my dad was attacked, I ran away. From all of them."

"You became an anonymity," I said softly, remembering

— 131 —

what *The Blood Texts* had said. "You became a ghost."

"Yeah, well, you have to learn how to be dead first. Things went wrong, I got found out. Probably I wanted to be. But both times I did, the kind people who got involved were attacked themselves. *That'll be Dad,* I thought. *If I get taken back, that'll be my dad.* So I learnt how to hide properly."

"Olivia, I'm so—" I began, but she cut me off with a shrill voice.

"Only you can't hide, can you, when you're being good? People resent you. You be nice, you don't judge, or brag . . . Still they resent you. Everywhere I went I would try to avoid attention, and everywhere bullies like you would wriggle out like *maggots*. And the elf *loved* that."

"He's insane," I said softly.

Olivia clapped her hands and laughed – a harsh, unhinged sound.

"Top marks for Evangeline Clark! Do ya *see* what you can do when you put your mind to it?! Yes, clever clogs, that elf is insane. It's version of good is impossible. It doesn't just hate bad behaviour; it *longs* for it. You saw it punishing Miss Faith – it *enjoyed* that. You can hold it back, sometimes. But it's *exhausting*. I was exhausted, protecting people who were making my life hell."

"Like me," I whispered. Olivia's face contorted suddenly, twisted with hate and fear, and I thought of Mum seeing the woman she'd once bullied in the shops, the woman flinching like she'd seen a big spider.

"You, Evangeline . . ." Olivia hissed. "You hurt me the

most. When I first arrived, I was so *lonely*. And you asked me to partner up on that family tree presentation for History and I . . . I couldn't believe it! You seemed so popular, and like an *idiot* I imagined that you might want to be my friend! For one lovely day, I pretended that I could *have* friends. I'd keep you safe, I'd keep away when you did bad things, and when you were good, we'd hang out. OK, so it was stupid – the whole point of the presentation was to arrange a family tree and I couldn't even tell you about my family! But then . . ."

Olivia faltered. Her face fell into a *horrible* dismayed expression, making her both younger and older.

"But then you never really asked about my family anyway. I was so *stupid*. You kept giving me that smirk when I tried to joke, and you kept wrinkling your nose when I leant closer, and I would run to the toilets and just *wash* and *wash* thinking *don't mess this up, don't lose your friend!* but it was just a thing you were doing, wasn't it? Like, a bit, for Kelsey and Declan? And then you did that stupid presentation saying my family were all serial killers and . . . and . . ."

I didn't have a word to say back. Olivia took a breath, composed herself.

"That's the thing with you bullies," she continued. "You all think you're the funniest, or the meanest. *Check ME out, I'll go there when nobody else will!* But you're fucking *everywhere*, you're fucking *bland*. You say the same things, and play the same tricks, and you *hurt* people. It's the easiest thing in the world to do, it's just, just . . . this . . . crap . . . *evil*."

"I'm not evil," I muttered desperately. "I'm not."

"No," Olivia said. "You're worse. You *can* be good and you choose not to be. Why? Are you *scared* of getting bullied yourself or something?"

I shrugged, and set my face. I honestly didn't know, but this was tough, like looking into a vicious mirror.

"Whatever the reason," she continued. "The day when you tripped me in the canteen, I couldn't take any more – I ran back here to the Derelicts. But then I heard your dad talking about you, and I couldn't believe it . . . it was too perfect! The father of my tormentor is here, working in my hideout, and not only is he Christmas crazy but he's fuming because his daughter is a bully! Carefully, I left the elf out right where your dad could find it, with strict instructions. Part of me felt terrible, what if the elf attacked your family? But mostly I just hated you *so* much, nothing else mattered. Can you imagine how gutted I was to visit the next day and see you there without even a scratch? What did you do that was so good? What made the elf hold back?"

"My mum said some things to me," I said. "I was already in trouble, wasn't I? And then . . . I deleted the photograph. I wasn't lying when I said I had."

"Do . . . do you want me to feel *grateful*?!" Olivia said, sneering. I shook my head but didn't dare speak. She was so *angry*, it was like she was clinging to her sanity by her fingertips. And what she said next made me wonder if she'd already let go.

"So I tried to give the elf to you."

"To . . . give him to me."

"Exactly! All this time I'd been followed around by this . . . this *curse*, this *monster*. All this time I'd been trying to hold it back, to stop it attacking, and when you were *so* mean that I actually sent it after you . . . it hadn't done a thing! What if, then, I could somehow pass the curse on to you? Make you responsible for the elf?"

"The elf wouldn't ever go for me," I said. "I'm not good enough."

"No, you're not," Olivia said, matter-of-factly. "It seemed like a crazy idea, but I could also tell that you were trying to pretend to be good – so hard, that for one night you had fooled the elf himself. The minute I thought of this plan, it seemed perfect. I would stuff the elf into my rucksack, bring him with me to the park, and when nobody was watching I'd attack you. Either the elf would help you out, and attack me – which would mean I was finally free and he was your problem . . . or you'd fight back and the elf would attack you. Win win!"

She burst out laughing at this, shrill and deranged. I felt sick, but also I felt guilty. I'd hurt this girl so much she'd lost her mind with hatred.

"Only one problem," Olivia continued. "Your brother turned up! And, as much as I hated you, I couldn't bring myself to get him hurt as well. But just as I was cursing my luck, that Harry boy he was with started to lose it and I had an idea. I didn't have to abandon my plan, but I might be able to make it foolproof. What was it you said that day?

'I'm turning over a new leaf'? Some stupid crap you bullies come out with every so often. I knew it wouldn't last, but if you could keep it going for a few days while the elf was still with you, I could do lots of small, sly things to mess with your life. Then, when I did get to attack you, I could tell you and the elf all the things I'd done, and surely then he would have to attack me and join you!"

I reeled back, all the nightmarish things that had gone wrong in the past two days spinning through my head.

"So . . . *you* sent Kelsey that message from my phone? *You* told everyone I'd attacked Miss Faith?"

"I'd even taken your reading book before your detention," Olivia said flatly. "Don't hope that I'll feel bad."

There were angry yells from the boys smoking outside, yells that turned to screams. *The elf*, I thought, but Olivia didn't move and neither did I.

"I don't understand how you could want to be attacked by that thing," I said softly. "When it went for Miss Faith it . . . it was horrifying. The kind of thing that ruins your life."

"What life?!" Olivia said, and she *wilted*, tears flooding her tired eyes. It was like all the anger had finally leaked out of her, leaving her with nothing but sadness. She gestured around her. "Look! Look! Anything is better than this. I can't . . ."

Just then, the streetlights flickered against the boarded-up window. Downstairs, the front door slammed. My phone torch began to spit like a dying candle, as those dreadful steps scurried up the stairs. All the while I stared at Olivia.

She had tried to give me a terrible gift. She had lied about me, had messed up my whole life. And *still* I couldn't say I didn't deserve it.

Paddapatatatarata...

Olivia's shoulders slumped. Despair filled her tired and tortured face. Mum's words came to mind.

If you get any chance at all to undo a bad thing you've done to Olivia, then you should jump at it. Because it's those missed chances that keep me up at night.

And I made a decision.

"You asked me," I said quietly. And Olivia looked suddenly confused.

Patatataratatatatap...

"You asked me," I said again, louder, and the footsteps ceased. "You asked me to put that photograph on the screen."

Olivia frowned. Then her exhausted eyes met mine, and they flickered with comprehension ... with hope.

"Do you know what that means—" she began, but I cut her off.

"You asked me to put that photo up so the elf would attack me," I continued. "*And* you sent that message to Kelsey. Just to get me hurt – what the hell is *wrong* with you?!"

There was a low growling sound. The streetlight and my phone torch, they both flickered one last time and illuminated the room. The elf was there, out in the hallway behind Olivia. He was staring at me, blood dripping from his snarling mouth.

"I did," Olivia said, her voice croaky and weak. "I did it."

Even now she struggled to lie.

"You put that picture of yourself up there," I repeated. "You sent that message to Kelsey to get me beat up. You took my reading book out, to get me in trouble. You smirked at Harry to wind him up. And you smirked about me, when Miss Faith made that joke about me."

"I did."

The elf stepped forwards, still staring at me. His growl grew louder and I couldn't help but step back, towards the window.

"You did all that. You asked for it. Whatever happens, you asked for it."

"I did," Olivia said, louder this time.

But it was too late. The elf moved towards me.

"Please . . ." I gasped, my courage failing at last. And with a snarl it LEAPT—

chewing . . .

scratching . . .

furious . . .

"*Ugh*," Olivia said, and I opened my eyes. I was unharmed, and the elf . . . the elf was snarling in the corner, biting at Olivia's face, her neck, her shoulder – those hideous claws tearing at her. Olivia wasn't screaming, but pain twisted at her tired face. There was the sound of lapping blood, of skin being sliced . . .

"Stop," I begged, but the elf didn't stop.

"*STOP! STOP! STOP!*"

Suddenly, the elf stopped, looking at me, breathing hard.

I locked eyes with it, feeling the force of that rage, that fanatic's sense of justice. And I didn't give in.

See, I'm brave at things like this, I know I am. When it counts, I'll just put my fears to one side and act.

"STOP," I said again. "It isn't right. You have to stop."

The elf watched me, still breathing hard, anger and *longing* playing with its hideous face. Slowly, surely, never tearing my eyes away from his, I stepped forwards. The elf let go of Olivia and she fell, unconscious and bleeding, to the floor.

"Come," I said. Then, slowly but surely I moved to the door. I walked across the landing. I stepped down the stairs, being careful not to trip. And I left through the front door.

I didn't look back till I was down the street. The elf was following me now.

— Epilogue —

I wish I could say that I ran away that night, but I didn't. It took one week, one desperate week, for the elf to attack my family – my sister, to be precise. I still fill with sadness whenever I think of the last time I saw her. That night, with my parents in the hospital, I left a note promising them that I'd be fine and please, *please*, don't worry about me. I don't think they will follow that advice.

Olivia was right, about a lot of things. It takes a lot to become a real ghost, especially when you're a kid. There's a lot of good people out there who mess things up with their worry and their care, and it's so easy to let them. I think about that first teacher a lot. I hope he's OK now.

There were these girls at the last school who didn't like me. I could tell it straight away. One of their boyfriends looked like Declan, and I kinda made the on-purpose mistake to flirt with him in the same way. I think they would have started on me sooner or later, but I definitely made it sooner. They began with small things – things left smeared in my bag, trips in the hallway. Then one of them texted me, asking if I wanted to hang out in the playing fields after school.

When I got there, the gang was waiting for me . . . and a load of other kids all ready to film the slaps.

I'm different to Olivia like that. These kids hadn't been my friends. And I've done good things before, but I've been fine being bad as well. I didn't feel a bit bad about what happened next.

After that, I had to disappear again though. I missed my parents a lot by then, that kind of pain in your stomach that just won't go away. I was tired, and I was cold. My feet hurt and as I got off the train at the next town along, I didn't know how much longer I could take of this. Once, I made the mistake of logging into my old GroupMe. There was a message from Edie.

> Don't know if you'll get this sis, but I've found some answers in the magicka. Tell me where you are and I'll save you.

Huh, some little kid's made-up 'Magicka'. I didn't dare go on GroupMe after that, just in case I got tempted to tell her where I was and put her in danger. Those days afterwards were the *hardest*.

That's when I saw Olivia. I'd just arrived in a new place when I saw her. She was walking out of Maccy's with a friend. A man called to her. He looked anxious *af*, there were deep shadows under his eyes and his cheeks were puffy, like he cried a lot, but then Olivia smiled and said goodbye to her friend and the man *beamed* with joy – I mean like *sunbeams* were pouring out of his face. There was a long scar along Olivia's cheek, the elf's parting gift. I wondered if anybody teased her about it, although she looked happy.

She was just about to turn away, when she saw me. She froze, her eyes boring into mine from across the junction. Then, very briefly, she nodded recognition. I nodded back. And before her face could slip to show fear, or dread, or anything that might hurt, I turned away and headed back to the train station.

That meeting will hopefully give me strength for a couple of towns, at least.

-About the author-

Frank Cadaver was born in the witching hour, beneath a blood-red moon, and under a bad sign. His first words were not fit to print. Now he scratches stories with yellowed fingernails, across the mouldering walls of the abandoned nuclear power station he calls home. If you like what you read, we'll dare you to find out more ...

Coming soon . . .

UNCLE ZEEDIE

2025

—— Preview ——

"Thank god for that, we're here," Dad muttered, and Lacey climbed out of the car.

Uncle Zeedie was stood by his front door. He'd barely changed. His skin was pale and plasticine, his dark hair as short and correct as a Lego piece, the eyebrows beneath it thin and sharp. His face was almost unreal, like a generic avatar from a video game. Except, maybe, this time, was his face a bit more lined? Was there more stubble on his plasticky skin than she remembered the last time? It didn't help the uncanny valley one bit. It just made him look like a doll with an infection.

It wasn't a nice thought, and Lacey told herself off for having it, but . . . but Uncle Zeedie didn't step forwards to greet them, but just stood there, rigid and tense, his hands tightly clasped, the smile on his face as forced and uneasy as rigor mortis. Not for the first time, she wondered.

Does he even want us here? He must do, else he wouldn't invite us, right?

Then why doesn't he ever show it?

"Hey, Uncle Zeeds," she said, a bit awkwardly.

"Hello, Larissa," Uncle Zeedie replied in his correct, high voice. Urgh, Lacey hated that name. She didn't run forward to hug him. It was just one of those things they knew, an unwritten rule you didn't need to say out loud. Don't hug Uncle Zeeds. Don't even shake hands, he doesn't like to be touched. Instead she stared at him, and he stared back. Twenty seconds and this was already proper awkward.

"Where is George?" he added finally.

"I . . . where is George?" Lacey's dad said.

———————

George was still in the car. He hadn't even undone his seatbelt. The Feeling had come back just a couple minutes earlier, you see.

It had first hit two minutes before, when the car had turned onto Uncle Zeedie's long, uneven drive. That curdling taste had struck the back of George's throat like COVID, and as they drove further along his mouth had flooded with hot, thick saliva, so much that he was sure he would be sick. He'd lied to himself like he always did, you're just too hot, you're nervous, you're tired, but he knew what it was. It was The Feeling.

George held his breath, and turned and stared hard out of the window so his sister and his dad wouldn't notice anything wrong. At first, the view had helped. Uncle Zeedie's swimming pool was out there, its underwater lights winking in the early dusk, the tennis courts a bit beyond it, and the woods, the woods were . . .

It was never a good idea to look too hard when The Feeling hit.

The woods around Zeedie's house were as wild as a rabid dog. The trees were overgrown and sun-starved, their gnarled branches curling up like arms thrown up to beg, beg for food. Even worse, the gaps between the trees were shadowed in a murky grey, glimpses of a foul, bubbling reality behind all of this money and luxury. George's eyes flitted from dark space to dark space, past the swimming pool, the tennis courts, past the boy with blood and . . .

[—bad here there's bad here there's bad here there's]

. . . NO!

George still hadn't spoken, but inside he'd screamed. He didn't want to look back at what he thought he saw, but he made himself look, his eyes darting back to where the boy covered in blood had just been.

It was all right. There was nothing there. The boy had gone. The thudding in George's ears died down, and as the car turned and slowed to a halt, he felt the seatbelt biting into his clenched hands.

"Thank god for that, we're here," Dad muttered, and the door opened. George didn't get out yet, didn't even let go of the seatbelt. But he breathed, once, twice. For a minute he'd been sure. For a minute he'd known. The Feeling had told him, that there was evil in this place. But The Feeling had been wrong before. It was probably all in his head. He breathed again, three times, four times.

That's when he heard the second breath behind him. It rasped, it gurgled, a throat filled with fluid. And the boy behind him said . . .

"Run."

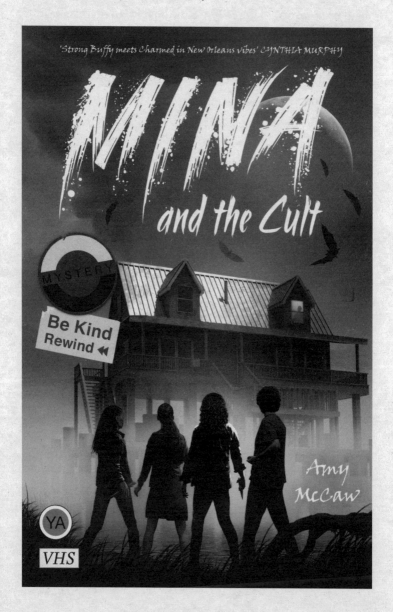

'Strong Buffy meets Charmed in New Orleans vibes' CYNTHIA MURPHY

MINA
and the Cult

MYSTERY

Be Kind
Rewind ◀◀

Amy
McCaw

YA

VHS

Danny Weston

INCHTINN

ISLAND OF SHADOWS

With interior
illustrations by
Miranda Harris

HAVE YOU EVER WONDERED
HOW BOOKS ARE MADE?

UCLan Publishing is an award winning independent publisher specialising in Children's and Young Adult books. Based at The University of Central Lancashire, this Preston-based publisher teaches MA Publishing students how to become industry professionals using the content and resources from its business; students are included at every stage of the publishing process and credited for the work that they contribute.

The business doesn't just help publishing students though. UCLan Publishing has supported the employability and real-life work skills for the University's Illustration, Acting, Translation, Animation, Photography, Film & TV students and many more. This is the beauty of books and stories; they fuel many other creative industries! The MA Publishing students are able to get involved from day one with the business and they acquire a behind the scenes experience of what it is like to work for a such a reputable independent.

The MA course was awarded a Times Higher Award (2018) for Innovation in the Arts and the business, UCLan Publishing, was awarded Best Newcomer at the Independent Publishing Guild (2019) for the ethos of teaching publishing using a commercial publishing house. As the business continues to grow, so too does the student experience upon entering this dynamic Masters course.

www.uclanpublishing.com
www.uclanpublishing.com/courses/
uclanpublishing@uclan.ac.uk